Darkness in a Sky of Embers

By Catori Sarmiento

Three Ravens Publishing
Chickamauga, GA USA

This book is dedicated to active duty members and

veterans of the military.

A sincere thanks goes to my second cousin, Ruby

Cofer, who I hope becomes a successful writer.

1

Soft snow fell quietly from the sky. Snow. In July. Or what Madeline thought was snow. It was white, soft, and drifted through the air like candy tufts. It was a welcome interruption from her summer school class where she endured endless desk-sitting while trying to focus on a sheet printed with uninteresting multiple-choice questions. The other students in her class rushed towards the window, along with Madeline. When she looked out, some of her classmates were already outside playing in it. Her unease at the oddity was tempered by curiosity. She watched the tufts land atop a dandelion cluster, caking the yellow petals. The grooves in the leaves began to curl inward towards the stem. Others twisted and turned inside-out as if an invisible hand tormented it at the roots. It was then that they changed. The petals coiled inwards as a rotten black seeped through the once vibrant green.

A low rumble made Madeline turn to the sky. A gargantuan object larger than a thunder cloud shimmered in the light and turned the sheen of onyx when it changed direction. She looked back to her schoolmates who were now curled on the ground, their arms and legs bent and contorted. She squinted to see one of their faces. Shriveled and inhuman, his skin dissolved to reveal the muscle below. It was raw and red, like fresh cut liver. In the distance, she saw dark masses floating down in a silently elegant but malicious dance. They were not unlike giant jellyfish that drifted aimlessly in the sea. It was a deceptively beautiful sight that made her venture closer to the window even as the others retracted.

There was a terrible silence, like the moment between breaths, between the mind deciding which emotion to feel. There was a classmate she recognized. He was lying on the ground, on his side, as if he collapsed from exhaustion. His entire body convulsed. Blue electrical pulses flashed from under his skin. Its flesh was covered in boils, mouth drooping open, its eyes white, and all of it covered in a strange moist sheen. What were once fingers elongated into quivering tentacles that erupted with fleshy spines. The bubbling skin intensified, contorting what remained of her classmate's face.

She was afraid and she could not tear her eyes away.

That vision of her dissolving classmate and of the monsters descending from overhead intruded upon her as she attempted to sleep within the confines of the transport. She was squished against a number of other soldiers inside a warbling cargo plane. They were all so much older than her. Adult faces, men with shadows of facial hair, women with high cheekbones, their uniform ranks brazen on their chests and shoulders. Most of them slept. She did not know how they could. Madeline was abuzz with uneasy excitement. In a few hours, she would be in a war zone. She would fight *them*. She *would* be in control.

Madeline looked over her crisp beige and green camouflage uniform and fidgeted with the rank pin on her lapel. The two bronze chevrons signified her role as Engineer. She tugged at the combat patch on her right shoulder to ensure it had been sewn on securely. The patch had a three finned bomb in the center and crossed in the background by two lightning bolts proclaimed her completion of training and her acceptance into the Ordnance Corps. Madeline absentmindedly stroked the worn leather pocket knife case on her belt. Inside was a folding knife made with turtle shell inlay at the base and ivory at the hilt, the designs that were once carved there faded to all but a few lines of indentation. It was one of the few family mementos she was able to keep. At one time, it had been her grandfather's, then her father's, and now Madeline's.

She pulled back the sleeve at her wrist to check her watch. Madeline had not owned a watch before but purchasing one had been on her required list of items needed for deployment. It was practical. A field watch with a large face and sturdy wristband was all she needed. The time marked three hours since she boarded the transport with one more hour until they landed. She smoothed her sleeve down.

Her sights turned to the people around her. Though the enlistment age had lowered to fifteen, she had not yet met any other soldier close to her age. They were all older by at least a few years. Madeline settled her focus on an older woman who chewed on a piece of gum. She stifled a laugh. The way the older woman's chin moved reminded her of a goat chewing cud.

"You're one of the up-jumped troops," she accused. "The enlistment extension program?"

"Yes!" Madeline answered promptly. Then she noticed the woman's rank: two black chevrons topped with a bronze eagle with outstretched wings that denoted her superiority as a Specialist. "Yes, ma'am," Madeline added.

It had been essential to memorize the strict chain of command hierarchy. At the lowest point for enlisted members was Technician, then Engineer, followed by Specialist, and Sergeant. For the officers there was Lieutenant, Captain, Major, Colonel, Commander, and then the higher echelons of Field General, General, and Defense Force General.

Often, Madeline noticed the rank before the name. She checked the woman's name tape: Dubrovin. The woman raised her eyebrows high on her forehead. Madeline had seen her mother make the same expression and it usually meant that she did not believe whatever fib Madeline was telling.

"Good luck," she said unemotionally.

"Thank you," Madeline replied.

"*How* long was your training, exactly?" Dubrovin asked.

"Two weeks," she replied proudly.

The woman scratched her bottom lip.

"Is that all it takes to become a soldier now? Two weeks?"

Balking at the insult, Madeline became defensive.

"I'm just as good as anyone else here," she said.

"And what makes you think that?" Dubrovin retrieved a pack of gum, a new piece, and spat out her old gum in the new wrapper.

"I--" Madeline started.

"No," the woman interceded with a hand wave, "I know sardines like you. I was like that myself when I joined, so take it from me: You think you might be a hero. What is that, really? It's never how you think it'll go."

Madeline was insulted that the woman misjudged her so quickly.

"I don't want to be a hero," she said. "I just want to kill as many as I can."

Dubrovin laughed. In her smile, Madeline noticed the woman's teeth; the front canine displayed a noticeable break that left the tip blunt.

"Now *that's* the right reason to be here."

She recalled the object she had seen in the sky in her childhood. The one she had since learned about in her military training. There was something she wanted to ask, but hesitated a moment, reconsidered, and then blurted, "Have you seen a Damocles Spear?"

The old woman made a guttural noise that could have been a clearing of her throat or a grumble of disapproval.

"Now that's a thing you don't never want to see."

The old woman extended her arm, pulled back the long uniform sleeve, and turned her wrist to look at the watch face. It was an antique analog watch with a winding mechanism, and a hard steel casing.

"Maybe I do," she muttered, assuming the ambient sounds of the airplane would cover the possible insubordination.

There could be no doubt of the terrifying presence of the Helgrammaw. She had seen them when the Ashfall came. That single day which caused humanity's upheaval. The day when the creatures arrived. Morbid curiosity made her want to see them again, with her own eyes, and kill them.

It would begin soon.

2

The transport landed just outside Camp Ripley, Minnesota. The base had once been dedicated to military training during more peaceful times. As the war dredged on, it transitioned to a forward operating base where the military provided tactical support and secured the hostile area. It was far enough from the invisible influence of the creatures. If human technology reached too near to the Helgrammaw, it would gradually, assuredly, fail. It also meant the tedium of having to be driven from their drop point to the base.

She stepped out to where the sudden freezing air shocked her every bone. Though she wore fleece to cover herself against the weather, it was as if there were nothing to shield her from the blinding cold that hung in the air. It was the bleakest night where the stars were obliterated from the sky; muted out by the clouds that covered the expanse.

Yet, in the distance she saw the familiar phosphorescent aurora and the hints of inhuman undulations in its atmosphere. She knew them by a dozen different names. Each person had their own understanding of what to call them: things, demons, creatures. The Helgrammaw were their defined name.

The first she'd heard of the name was during training in a fill in the blank study guide of relevant terms.

The elevation brought on a high feeling of dizziness, and her breath worked harder to fuel her lungs with oxygen. Yet even in the darkness she could see the reflection of the crescent moon in the sky hidden softly behind the mountains where the tops were covered with bright snow. In the fluorescent lights that stood around every section of the base, she could see the tops of the buildings were scattered with snow, glowing bright white with the aid of the lights overhead. She stepped down from the airplane.

The rest of the troops disembarked from the transport, some sluggishly lugged their duffle bags, while others unloaded as quickly as possible and sprinted across the tarmac to the line of vehicles waiting for them. The vehicles were old military trucks with a canvas cover above the flat bed. Madeline ducked her head under the canvas to get in and sat amongst the same passengers as before. A few removed their wireless phones, thumbed the number pad, or tried to dial. Some were lucky and picked up a signal and others continually tried and failed.

The next stop was the main base. They were dropped off in front of a nondescript square building with only a number to identify it. Everyone got out, Madeline followed. They all knew what she did not: the wordless process that channeled a soldier into service. None of this had been explained to her, that she remembered.

Inside the building was a single desk and a fatigued young man who sat behind it. He had a desktop computer, and shallow mesh trays stacked with paperwork. One by one, each troop removed their orders, handed them to the man, who spoke briefly, and then left. Madeline placed her sea bag on the floor. She had stowed them away in her binder after using them to get on the transport. She heard a man chuckle at her.

"Better not put those away until you leave this place."

Madeline did not like how he laughed at her.

"Well, I didn't know that," she said, rustling through her bag to fondle around inside to feel where it had shifted during the flight. When she felt the edge, she picked it up with her thumb and forefinger, and pulled it out the open top. With it came a pair of her fluffy rainbow unicorn bed socks. A gift from her sister before she left. She looked around briefly as she stuffed them back in to make sure no one had been drawn to the juvenile clothing. Fortunately, most were too focused on getting in and getting out to tease her about it. When she re-closed the top and rose, she had seen that the man behind her had skipped her in the line, including the others behind her, who bypassed where she stood.

Madeline walked up the stairs and into her dorm room which she, thankfully, had to herself. The room smelled of age with the congealed scent of too much use, much like a hotel room which always carries the smell of too many bodies. It was barely furnished; a shaded window that looked down on the tan outer wall of one of the buildings, an outdated television, a floor lamp, a bed with a naked mattress, and a bedside table. Her sights stopped at the table. On it was a well-used black rotary dial telephone and a book. The telephone was something she had seen in a museum once and she had not seen a physical reading book for some time.

She picked it up. The cover worn, corners soft, fuzzy from use, the title faded but legible, with striped colors on the cover. The binding was loose but had double-backed black electrical tape that someone had used to attempt to repair it. She opened it to flip through colorful pages of Seussian characters: a children's book.

Thinking it a disparaging prank, she shut the book and placed it in the drawer.

The room was just as cold as the air outside of it, kept frozen with the emptiness of being unoccupied. There was a small thermostat next to the door which she promptly turned on. She dropped her bags on the floor by the door, rummaging through the duffle bag to find the fluffy socks that she suddenly appreciated for their usefulness. She took off her boots and wool socks. After wiggling her toes and picking out some wooly fluffs, she slipped the comfortable socks on and collapsed onto the unmade bed, careful to set the alarm on her watch for seven o'clock—in two hours—for her to meet with her unit sergeant. She settled into the bed, attempting to find comfort, like a mouse burrowing into a soft nest. She closed her eyes against the cold and waited as the heater murmured into life and blew warm air into the confines of the room. After only mere moments of finally falling into a light sleep, the alarm beeped against her ear. Though her window shades were closed, she could make out the peeking sunlight behind them. She stretched her arms above her head in the air that had warmed while she slept and she cursed the unfortunate requirement that she had to meet her sergeant so early, wishing she could instead immediately go to work.

Nevertheless, she pulled herself up from the single mattress bed. She tried the television, which worked in the sense that it turned on and displayed channels. Yet, the reception was flippant. One channel might work for a time, become static, and restart at a delayed pace, others were twitchy, or else had unsynced audio. She turned it off and went to her duffle bag where she kept her issued gear. She pulled a large, hooded camouflage jacket from it and wrapped her arms through it. With her paperwork in hand, she went outside and exposed herself to the blinding sunlight of the frozen morning. Tiptoeing mindfully down the slippery steps, she planted her feet firmly onto the rocky ground. There were patches of snow in the areas of shade surrounding the outlines of the buildings and branching outwards until the sunlight overhead squelched it. Many of the area buildings were the remains of decades old warehouses, having since been overtaken by the conglomerate of troops. Other areas were in the process of re-building, as part of the base expansion to solidify the presence of the ever-growing military. The entirety of the base was like a shanty town, with reminders of eras built atop each other. Some buildings were dilapidated wood, others not buildings at all but portables, still more were a newer tan with brown numbers painted on the sides. When she found the area that housed the Ordnance Division, she was surprised at its ramshackle stature. She expected something else, something pristine, state-of-the art, like she had seen in the movies.

The walls of the building were of thin maple wood, sanded down to give off a lighter color. Some were nailed together to form the closing walls of open offices where desks stood with unused computers on top. In the main room was an old flat screen television screwed into the center of the wall and two flags on pedestals in the corner: one American and the other Canadian. Spread out onto one of the adjacent walls was an area map with multicolored tacks pressed against it; each color representing varying categories of Mites. Hanging from the center point of the ceiling was a roll of fly paper already stuck with half a dozen flies.

Through the main area was a wooden door with a brass knob, propped open to reveal an office behind it. When she walked through the shop, her boots made a shallow noise against the wooden floor. Her footsteps must have revealed her presence, for a lone uniformed woman who was in one of the closer offices stepped out to see her. Noticing Madeline's unit badge at once, she held out her hand to shake it.

"You must be one of the relief," she said.

Madeline nodded.

"I'm Sergeant James. Just get in?"

"Yeah. Madeline," she began, by habit, then corrected herself, "Engineer Yazzie. I was task promoted just before coming here," she said, with a failed attempt at battening her pride.

"Yes, I heard," she said. "I've tried to tell them about that virtual training, but the schoolhouse just won't listen to me. Lowering the enlistment age and throwing out these task promotions like candy are no test for the real thing. I hope you do not think that just because you exploded a few game sprites that that prepares you for what happens here. Do you even know how to drive?"

The way she asked caused Madeline to scoff at the insult. "I can drive," she said proudly. "I got my license two years ago."

Her superior blinked slowly. She drew a breath as if searching for patience.

"So, Sergeant James. Do you have a first name?"

Sergeant James looked at her incredulously. "Not on the job, I don't. I wouldn't worry about first names."

Madeline decided to change the subject.

"What's it like here?' She asked.

The woman took a long pause before answering. Madeline's eyes rose sharply to meet her and the apprehension on the sergeant's face told Madeline everything.

"It's busy. You'll see how it is. There's a lot going on all the time. It can get a little crazy. You've got those *Mites* out there--"

"Mites?" she interrupted.

The sergeant paused at the interruption, leaned back, raised her chin, and locked eyes with Madeline. "Helgrammaw is a mouthful. Easier to say 'Mites'."

She had only seen them in briefing pictures. Those were the enemies fought by the ground troops, and so she was relieved that she may never have to see them. The worst of them were human, once, perhaps still, but had been transformed so that the entirety of their bodies were covered in what looked like large, gelatinous boils that could be used to camouflage into the surroundings and emitted pulses of blue bioluminescence when disturbed. Calling them "Mites" seemed counter-intuitive.

"But they don't look anything like that," Madeline said.

"It's what we've always called them." Sergeant James shrugged a shoulder. "Anyway, there aren't many of us around lately. Most of the teams left out of here a week ago and we're just getting some new ones in the past few months. I arrived here myself about a week ago." She scratched a patch of psoriasis on the back of her hand. "So, since you're an Engineer, you'll have two troops under you, Goodway and Rostein." Madeline perked at the possibility of being a leader, until she added, "I don't think you'll have to worry. They can take care of themselves." She paused, turned her ear to the back wall, and said, "I think the captain's free now. Show time tomorrow, well, unless you get a call, is five at the armory."

Madeline's eyes widened at the hour. "Kind of early, isn't it?"

"This is why I keep telling them--" she murmured to herself, closed her eyelids, mumbled, then looked at Madeline. "There's no 'early'. Early makes it seem like we have normal hours. It's just sleep and work. Here, I'll take you over." She stood up and walked out, not waiting.

Madeline passed through the threshold of the Flight Sergeant's office to another nondescript office just beside it. Captain Green was the name and rank written in permanent marker on a piece of wood that had been nailed just eye-level on the wall by the door. The sergeant opened the door. A man with darkened skin and two silver bars pinned on his collar stood up to greet her. The man smiled and shook her hand immediately, showing her immense gratitude for the presence of another body.

"The newbie! Thanks for being here," he said and gestured to a chair, "have a seat."

Madeline sat in the worn chair while her unit sergeant did the same.

"We're spread pretty thin," he began without ceremony, "like usual. So, you're going to be in with one of the teams. We have three here and we go out with the other ground force units sometimes for route clearance or if they find some cache. For sure, you'll be busy here." He paused to open his desk drawer and remove a file folder along with a thick white binder with severely worn edges.

"No computers?" she japed.

"Oh, we *have* computers," Sergeant James said, "Trouble is, they cut out half the time or the Mites interrupt the wireless signals."

"So," the captain continued, "Most of the reliable tech is all analog."

"Right." She thought of the phone in her room. "Is that why there's a weird phone in my room?"

"Weird?"

"Yeah, it has a wheel on it."

He laughed. "That's one way to describe it. I'm guessing you don't know how to use one."

She shook her head.

He turned around a similar phone on his desk.

"It's not surprising. I didn't either at first. These things are over seventy years old, but it was cheap to get them in surplus and they're reliable. So, this office number is five-six-six," He picked up the receiver and with his other hand, used his middle finger to place into the hole with the number five, then dragged it, the wheel making a *shhhring* as it rotated, and then stopped at the metal band. He then released his finger, letting the wheel reset, and repeated the same steps for the remaining numbers.

"Got it?" he asked. He turned the phone around again. "So, let me brief you a little."

The captain flicked open the binder, searching for a page, and once finding it he turned it to face Madeline. On two separate pages were pictures of what she would likely encounter in the field. Mites of all sizes and colors, some of which she had not seen before.

"You're young," he began. Madeline braced herself for what she thought would be a lecture or a reprimand like she had from the sergeant. "So, let me be clear that my expectations for you aren't any different from anyone else here."

Madeline relaxed. Fairness was her preferred medium. She hated when she had school classes where the teacher had clear favorites.

"Here's your tasker: More of these pop up every day, usually to gain more ground."

"Route clearance." Madeline said, remembering her training, to which he nodded.

"Just got to clear the way for the other troops coming through."

"That's all?" She asked.

He chuckled, revealing several crooked front teeth, one having a significant chip on the corner, and a distinctive overbite.

"'That's all'? Yeah. That's all. It's enough of a task that I have had to send home at least two dead or injured every few months," he said factually. Captain Green then folded his hands together. "Sound easy now?"

She was silent in response. He shut the giant binder which gave an audible thud.

"Well, you're still in-processing with us so I won't have you start anything until tomorrow. You'll work with a few others. . ." He thought for a moment, ". . . rotation teams. You'll be a more stationary team here."

"Sounds good."

"So! Go back and get some sleep and tomorrow meet up here at four thirty."

Madeline could not hide her emerging smile. Finally, she would get to join the fight.

"Great."

She pushed in her chair before leaving.

Once outside in the morning warmth, she noticed the flies. Tiny specks whirring around the empty space. When she walked, she disturbed some and had to flick them away. Returning to her room, she decided that she should wash her clothes. The last time they had been cleaned was during training. There, the laundromat had been used so often that she was hardly able to use a washer and dryer. On the off chance that she had, they were so overused that it would take hours to dry even the smallest load. Since then, she preferred to wash by hand and hang dry. As she scrubbed, rinsed, and wrung her clothes, she longed for the days when she could toss her soiled laundry into a washer, push a button, and let the machine do the hard work. How comforting it was, in its simplicity.

Madeline hung the damp clothes over the shower curtain rod. She shuffled into the room and fell on her bed, trying to coax herself back to sleep.

When she woke, she found the late daylight settled in her room and brought herself up, her head drowsy from such little sleep. She hoped it would have been morning already, but looking at her watch it was afternoon, and still the same day. It seemed so long already.

Somewhere nearby she heard the piercing revving of a UTAV, the Universal Tactical Assault Vehicle. It had been made for dual purposes. In the absence of Mites, it was a streamlined egg-shaped body with a raised cockpit at the rear and spheres underneath that allowed for sleek anti-gravity movement. When present, the creatures' interference would make the vehicle useless, so it had adaptive technology that allowed it to be driven manually. Madeline recalled her week of vehicle training where proficiency in driving both systems was necessary.

Madeline walked out into the dirt streets where she could see the base of the mountains uprooted from the mud, in the distance the ultraviolet sky that was enemy territory.

She walked along a single pathway with a row of vending machines that dispensed Amp Energy drinks, hot meals, and basic amenities. She passed a community center. She stopped at the door and turned to open it. Her hand slipped on the handle that was loose from wear. She had to use two hands to pull it open. Glancing inside, there was an old, musty stench that likely emitted from the low blue carpet covering the floor. Inside was a pool table where two young men in their military issued sweat wear played against each other. Farther in there was a wall lined with telephones. Although there were three of them, only one had a line of people waiting behind it.

Madeline closed the door and continued on. At the end was a large tent barracks where a line of uniformed people stood outside as those in the front perused a laminated food menu. The fresh smell of bread and sizzling meat wafted in the area, melding with the other fast-food counters and the steaming food from the chow hall. Her stomach was cramped with the need for food, and she found her way to the back of the line.

She noticed the man in front of her staring at his hand. Other than the odd plasticized sheen of his hand's flesh, she found the man's features unremarkable. He could easily fit in the place of one of the other men in line, like the patriotic men in recruitment advertisements. Where he stood out was in his presentation. His uniform was impeccable; neat creases in his sleeves and pants, with his cap fit snugly on his clean-shaven head. He then put his hand in front of his face, tapping each forefinger on his thumb, from the index to the pinky, and then in reverse, accelerating each time to the point where they became a flurry.

"Is that some kind of game?" Madeline asked.

"Nah," he said, without looking at her, "New hand."

He then turned to look at her, revealing a fresh, crescent scar from his temple to the top of his left ear, still pink, but sealed with shiny transparent glue.

"I was doing a patch job on the UTAV spinners and it spazzed—took my hand clean off. I thought they'd send me back home but turns out the medics here can fix you up." He laughed to himself. "I think this one's better than my old hand—can't wait to really test it out," he made his thumb and forefinger into the shape of an "O" and shook it back and forth, "You know?"

"Ah," she said, disappointment at his crudeness clear in her voice. She did not think adults would share the same low humor as boys she had known in school. She retorted, "Have you been waiting long to come up with that one?"

He flashed a grin that she supposed he thought was charming, but which to her appeared lascivious.

"Just for a pretty lady to show up."

She sighed. "No, thanks. I—"

He twisted his face into clear indignation, then scoffed. "Whatever. It was a joke. Lighten up," he said, then turned his back to her.

Her fists tightened. If it were not for the triple chevrons on his sleeve that indicated his higher rank, she would have swiped his hat and thrown it in the dirt. Much as she wanted to, she decided that the best course of action was to remain with her tongue pressed firmly to the roof of her mouth and her teeth gritted together.

The line moved at a slow pace. It was no different than waiting in the food line for every meal while she and her family were refugees. All those thousands of miles away, would her family be waiting in line, just as she was? She tried to push the thoughts deeper. She yawned. A fly landed on her hand that she brushed away.

The closer she came to the entrance, the stronger the smell, and the louder the sound of metal trays banging together. Eagerness closed the gaps in between each soldier. When it was her turn, she at first took one tray, but then, noticing the men in front of her taking two each, thought again, and decided to follow suit. More flies whizzed around, but she was too distracted by the food to care.

Steam rose from a single row of steel pans filled with food on the buffet counter. Madeline indiscriminately spooned each option onto her tray. There was the usual cheap food: baked beans, minute rice, three types of pasta, and then fuller meals of chicken steak, beef roast. When one was full, she filled the other tray, making sure to grab the prepackaged muffins, cookies, and sweetbreads that she stored in her pockets. At the end of the line, she used both hands to carry her trays carefully, looking around the open space of plastic benches and tables for a place to sit amongst the jumble of uniforms.

As she looked at all the adult faces, Madeline felt more isolated than she expected as she looked at her older comrades huddled together in their faded camouflage, worn boots, and tired faces.

It's nothing like those posters in the recruiter's office, she thought, remembering the motivational pictures of young, svelte soldiers in patriotic, pristine dress.

There was a loud murmur in the chow hall, each conversation mixed with bouts of laughter bounced off the walls. She found a sliver of an open seat on one of the benches crowded by soldiers. Her focus was solely on the food she was about to eat. She barely noticed the person she sat next to. As soon as she placed her tray down, and sat, she shoved the food into her mouth indiscriminately. It all tasted as delicious as a chain restaurant brunch. She paused to push a piece of grilled chicken to the inside of her cheek to let her stomach settle. She let out a constrained burp, which gained the notice of the soldier sitting next to her.

The soldier appraised her rank and chevrons and asked, "Ordnance Engineer, no?"

Madeline turned to see a man looking at her with lean features, red rims around his eyes, and splotchy bumpy patches on his neck and cheeks from shaving too closely. Madeline did not recognize the pale olive color of his uniform, the crossed key imagery on his patch, or the bronze chevron on his lapel. Her mouth was still full, so she nodded. Once she swallowed, she asked, "You?"

"Logistics and Mapping. *Armee de l'Air:* French Air Force."

"What're the French doing here?" she asked. Nothing in her training mentioned foreign armies.

The man shrugged. "For the same reason as the Canadians, I imagine." He paused to scratch his neck. "Ordnance," he said again, thinking, "we have to make your maps."

"It can't be that hard," she said, snacking on a piece of chicken.

"No, not hard; tedious. All the maps are digital, satellite. Well, we can't use that when the *meduses* swim in the air. So, we have to research the archives and print them. Unfortunately, that means they can be . . . not so accurate."

"Screwed up is more like it," said a woman across from them who was holding a disposable paper cup in hand and drank from it. Madeline recognized the combat patch on the right shoulder. A sword with the blade tip pointed skyward, impaling a serpentine dragon was the proud imagery worn by Combat Oversight.

"Pardon?"

"Last week we went out there with the wrong map--"

"--*Alor*. Not this again."

"--took a turn that was supposed to be a main road and ended up on some country back road full of Mites."

The man released an audible sigh. "This was discussed already with the commander. *That* was the map request that we got. It's not our fault that you went to the wrong place."

"*Your* bad map got three of us killed."

The man rubbed his forehead with two forefingers, then relaxed, "Listen," he said, "It's unfortunate that your friends died. Maybe next time have your driver learn to read a map."

The woman stood up suddenly, rustling the tableware as she did, and pressed her lips together. "Well, how would you know? All you do is sit in a back office all day."

The woman left, taking her cup with her. The man said nothing, though his face blushed pink with anger as he hit the end of the table with an open palm. Madeline, knowing better than to disturb an angry man, finished her food and departed. Returning to her room, she fell into a restless sleep.

3

The mornings were darker than she imagined; dark and silent. There were few birds to call upon the sunrise. Except for the hardiest of breeds, they had all disappeared with the Ashfall. There was a great wind that rushed over her skin, carrying the dying dirt with it in the air. The vast sky above her formed in clouds of darkness that swept towards them like a shadow over the ground, enshrouding and voiding the landscape of light. It was as if a massive hand enclosed itself on the world to shut out the brightness of the sun. It was a nightscape; a deception. The sun shone high somewhere above the muggy mist that hung in the air for hours

Eagerness made her insert her optic lenses. They fit so comfortably that she could easily forget about them. Little different from contact lenses, these were constructed with graphene imagery sensors, which allowed her to view the ultraviolet and infrared spectrum that the Helgrammaw traveled upon.

Anticipatory excitement kept her alert in the early dawn as she searched her way to the meeting point, getting turned around at points in confusion as all the buildings looked the same, until she found the Armory. She went inside. The officers were already there. Captain

Green had a can of Amp Energy in hand and his weapon slung across his chest as he stood chatting with one of the sergeants who had her arms crossed so Madeline couldn't see her name tape. The door opened quickly, hitting the outside wall, and a woman and a man entered. Both wore the Ordnance Corps patches. She assumed these were her troops: Rostein and Goodway.

"You're nearly on time," the captain said in Madeline's direction.

"Ready to go," Madeline responded.

Sergeant James raised her eyebrows as she glanced at Madeline. "Where's your gear?"

Madeline cursed out loud. She heard mild laughter from others.

"I'll--"

"--Hurry up."

She ran out, back to her room, all the while cursing at herself for being so obviously forgetful. Madeline grabbed all her gear, making sure to double-check that she had everything, then returned to the armory.

When she arrived, the rest of her flight was already outside.

"Get armed-up and meet us at the convoy," the sergeant said, pointing to the dirt parking lot a thousand yards away.

Madeline rushed to the nondescript building.

She waited in line behind the Oversight team, who each approached a barred window in the center of the room, there was a quick exchange of words, and each was given a weapon through the open slat. It reminded Madeline of waiting in a bank line. One of the men turned his gun muzzle-down, looked at the base, and groaned.

"What number this time?" another man in line asked.

"Eleven twenty-six," he answered.

"Better than three-fourteen," he answered.

When it was Madeline's turn, the man behind the bars, a young man, she noted, with the beginnings of a mustache growing in around his upper lip, and spots of acne on his chin, asked her for her weapons card.

"My what?" she asked.

He looked her up and down. "You from the schoolhouse?" he asked.

"Yeah."

"They should've given you one with your ID. D'you have that?"

Madeline went to the wallet in her inside blouse pocket. Keeping her personal information close was a lesson learned from living as a refugee after the creatures displaced her family.

She looked through her cards, her ID, military bank card, her old school ID, a folded-up picture of her family, and a pale green weapons card. She passed it to the man.

He checked it, looked down at something on the desk under the window, and gave it back to her, which she replaced quickly, and returned her wallet to its place.

"Sixteen, huh?" he asked.

"And?" she asked.

The young man shrugged. He turned around to the back wall lined with gun safes. What the men before her had said about the numbers made her worry that she might get a bad one. The man returned and passed the weapon to her. She checked the number at the base and walked off, upset. Behind her, she heard the next man ask what number she had and laughed when the armorer told him.

Madeline slung her weapon, hefted her gear, and met her flight at the convoy. No time was wasted reviewing the map. They would approach the area where there were reported Mites, cordon the area, and detonate. As if rehearsed, a team mobilized quickly where they would ride out in a convoy with Combat Oversight, ground soldiers who served as the sharp spotters.

Madeline tapped her toes against the inside of her boots. Her sights were drawn to a young man across from her who wore a pair of wide brimmed sunglasses. He brushed at a fly that landed on his nose, and then crossed his arms so she could not read his name tape. On one knucklebone was a tattoo of what looked like a letter, but one Madeline didn't recognize. She looked at the set of his eyes, the tone of his skin, the fullness of his lips.

"I remember you from one of the classes!" she said in hopes that he was a peer.

He gave a short smile that emerged as a parting of the right side of his lips, as if a fish hook caught on his bottom lip and the line was tugged downward. She recognized him suddenly.

"You were in Spatial Logistics with me. I remember seeing you."

"Not hard to miss the oldest one in the class," he said, then studied her for a moment. "Oh, yeah, I know you," he said, then after thinking for some time, added, "you asked a lot of questions. Made the classes go overtime."

"It was a pretty cool class," she said. Training and learning how to fight the Mites was the only experience of being thoroughly engaged in academics.

His eyebrows rose at her comment. Madeline noticed.

"Didn't you think so?" she asked.

"It was--" he started, then stopped when a metal can hit his shoulder. They both looked over to where it lay on the ground, a can of Amp Energy, and then to the person who threw it, a woman whose rank of Technician was just below Madeline and whose tag read "Rostein".

"Sorry," she said. "I thought you heard me call out."

Goodway picked up the can.

"Thanks, anyway. I'll drink it later."

"Is this the kid?" Rostein asked, pointing at Madeline.

"*Engineer* Yazzie," Madeline stressed.

Rostein put up her hands, showing her palms, as if in a feigned show of deference, and made a sarcastic expression.

"No argument from me," she said. "Anyone who volunteers to join this mess gets high marks in my book."

Madeline felt relief at her acceptance. She might come to like Rostein, after all.

"What's with the numbers?" Madeline asked. When Rostein asked for clarification, Madeline said, "The guys in the armory were talking about the weapon numbers,"

"Oh, *that*," Rostein said. "It's just the Grunt's superstition. They think some weapons are luckier than others."

The captain called them to attention.

"The tasker today is route clearance. Standard Protocol." He turned to Madeline. "Let's also welcome Engineer Yazzie and show her how it's done."

"Raw," Madeline said, "should be fun."

They each entered the vehicle with Rostein taking the driver's seat. Inside the vehicle was a compact space just enough to fit the five of them and a moderately sized tactical robot. There would be more room if not for the equipment and additional gear contained within compartments on the walls and ceiling. With each of them seated, Rostein engaged the navigation console screen with coordinate inputs from the captain. Though automated, there was still the ability to drive manually if there was a call for it. Considering that the various Mites could render their electronics useless, it was essential to have a viable manner of transportation.

While she watched the movement of the vehicles before her, she shifted her sights from the landscape, the edge of the road, her side mirrors, and the spotters atop the vehicles. It would be brazenly simple for Madeline to have become desensitized to it, to the shadow that cast upon her--upon them all--but she found that as she moved ever closer to the face of death, she saw the humanity of all in life and felt almost distanced from it, in a sense of purgatory that forced her to walk alongside destruction but always saw that her hands could remove the cause of death. Her sights remained ever forward with her head held straight and her eyes alert. They drove through the rocky road in a line of other similar vehicles; grit flew about the wheels as the tires gripped the shaky road. Madeline's mind was silent as Rostein and Goodway bantered and joked around her. Madeline preferred to remain quiet to absorb her new surroundings and position. It would take her some time before she would feel relaxed enough around to jest.

Coming upon the field of view was a wall of hovering masses. Their tentacles hung down, reaching the dirt below. Spines protruded from each tentacle forming claws at the end. The sheer scale immediately impressed upon her the seriousness of their cause. This was nothing like training.

Scanning, she counted more than fifty of them in a tight row, swaying slightly back and forth as if in a gentle current. The navigation screen began fluctuating, the picture blinked off and on from the effects of the electronic pulses. The UTAV pulled to a slow stop when she heard the call over her radio and the signaling from the spotter in the vehicle before her.

Madeline opened her breast pocket to remove her gloves and sheathed them over her hands in preparation. She jumped from the seat, careful to shift her weight correctly so she did not catch on any of the hardware inside of the vehicle. She next reached for the upper parts of the bomb suit on the wall.

"There's plenty of time," the sergeant said. "Eagerness contradicts the patience needed for this job. Don't forget that."

She grabbed the armored vest anyway.

"I don't want to waste time," she answered.

Rostein muttered what Madeline assumed was an insult. Madeline fumbled with the vest while she slipped it over her uniform.

"I hope this isn't the first time you've put this on," Goodway said.

She clipped the straps into place.

"*No,*" she answered, grabbing the next piece, "It's the second."

Madeline attached the remainder of the suit, standing at one point then crouching inside the vehicle to secure each piece. It was a heavy, bulky thing that added at least fifty pounds to her body, with a similarly heavy collar that dug into her clavicle. It was necessary to ensure as much protection as possible. If any part of a mite were to touch them on the skin it would be debilitating. She attached the helmet by shifting it into place until it clicked.

The Combat Oversight team dispersed around the area like a swarm from a hive. Captain Green waved down the leader, a hardened woman with a clean face and bronze skin. In the wake of so many interchangeable faces, she learned long ago to memorize others by their name tape and by the halves of their uncovered faces, the rest protected by black balaclavas. It was the older woman from the transport.

Madeline wanted to give a greeting but there was not enough time since Oversight moved to provide cover. With a signal from the captain, they went to work. It was a standard mobilization procedure. The captain supervised while the others removed the proper equipment from the vehicle. Each of them had a gear pack with the appropriate tools that they shrugged onto their shoulders. Sergeant James took to the front, carrying a case of explosives as if it were nothing more than a briefcase full of paperwork. It was a distance of two hundred meters that they had to cover as quickly as possible. At a safe proximity, their team stopped to recover and drink water, leaving Rostein and the sergeant to put on their own set of bomb suits then set up the explosives. Madeline and Goodway moved to position the blast shield, a flat object that unfolded into a multi-paneled protective screen.

Madeline stopped immediately at the sight of a pale, smooth, bulbous object sticking up from the ground. She pushed her communication button to notify the others that she was engaging then focused her enhanced vision on the fleshy mound. Madeline approached, then balked.

She saw the body of a child, bloated from death and half assimilated with bubbled skin and protrusions from its nose and mouth. She was thankful that the figure's face was to the dirt and she saw only a glimpse of the loose clothing on her body that made it recognizably human.

Though she turned her head from the body, it didn't stop the smell of rotten flesh that flowed on the breeze. She held her breath. Anything more would cause a churning in her stomach and surely she would vomit. None of the others said a word, though they all witnessed the body on the ground. The only signal of the abnormality was when Rostein held a hand up to her face to cover her mouth and nose from the smell and Goodway exhaled sharply. It was a smell not easily forgotten.

"We have work to do," Goodway said finally.

Madeline shook her head and breathed shakily. She hadn't seen a dead body like that before. She could linger on it, but Goodway was right. She turned to him and nodded.

"Yes, we do."

They stopped where the team of combat Engineers stood in their procession. Madeline surveyed the ground where a section of the sand had been swept away to reveal a mass beneath it. A dime sized portion that had not been properly covered reflected a small glint of sunlight. She knelt on the side and with a steady gloved hand she brushed away the remaining dirt until the surface of it was clear. There was the top of a Mite. It was black and undulating below the surface. The dummies they used in training did not look the same, she remembered. Those were lifeless, easy to manipulate, and mindless.

Mites are mindless too. The same as all of them, she thought, recalling her training modules.

She poked it with her gloved finger. A razor-sharp spine shot up to meet it, causing her to retract her hand immediately. Her heartbeat jumped. She checked her fingers. Though her gloves had protected her from injury, she stared at her hand as if it were not her own, and then at the creature.

God, this is the real deal, she told herself, grappling with reality.

The captain paced over to where she stooped, stopped, and carefully looked over her shoulder.

"Take care of it," he instructed.

Madeline exhaled in a cleansing blow. Rather than being squeamish, she was steadfast and gently put her metal detector down at her side. Madeline removed a remote kit from her vest pocket. With as steady a hand as she could muster, she attached the wire to the exposed top of the mite. Feeding out the length of wire she picked up the detector and kept walking backwards until she was a safe distance away. Madeline took her detector once more and heaved it up, to feed the wire back to where she had a charge ready. When she returned, she connected the wire to the charger.

"Fire in the hole! Fire in the hole! Fire in the hole!" she called out.

Madeline counted off steadily and pressed the button to the controlled detonation. There was one loud pop. To her it sounded like an exploding M80 on street pavement on the Fourth of July. A shower of disheveled soil at once flew into the air and descended to the ground. She waited, hoping some secret would emerge, some revelation as to their true nature. She peered closer at the scene where the only noticeable change was in the churned soil and lingering dust. The captain looked to Madeline and gave her a nod of approval, raising her confidence.

She and the others lined up and step by cautious step, scanned the area in front and around their position in a half circle.

A deep scream was the only sound. Madeline turned to see it was the woman, Dubrovin who was on the ground and screaming. Madeline ran to the woman amidst the *pop, pop, pop* of foot soldiers firing at the Mites, and the indiscriminate shouts from behind. When she reached the woman, she stood, dumbfounded, at the body laid bare before her.

There were *things* coming out of her open belly. Intestines wriggled from within the living carcass. Tendrils crept over her flesh, through tears in her uniform. They writhed their way up her neck toward her face. Dubrovin screamed, repeating the phrase, "I don't want to die. I don't want to die."

Madeline's lips pressed tightly together to hold in any noise that may escape. She wanted to help, but it happened so quickly. The woman's body changed. Entrails retreated, wrapped around themselves, and retracted inside. The rest of Dubrovin's skin metamorphosed. Madeline turned away. She couldn't watch any longer.

4

There was little that could be done to stop the metamorphosis except for a controlled explosion and even then, she would have to move quickly. Madeline took a smooth, white brick sized object from her utility belt. She quickly examined the standard issue stun device. Looking down at her arm control screen, she tapped at the controls. A red spot pulsated in the center.

She tossed it gently underhanded, so it landed near the changed woman. Madeline checked her watch for the time. She gave the warning and watched the hand count down from thirty seconds. They all tucked their chins down behind the raised armor, each one of them resembling defensive tortoises. Arming turned the pulse to green and after activation sent a concentration of toxins directly through the tactile subject, immediately paralyzing it.

That was the first step: stun and then disable. Careful to avoid the dangling tentacles, the explosives were set at two meters' distance in front and in a row of four set at a similar width. After the explosives were in place, they attached the detonation line to each set, trawling the line just behind the blast shield where they converged into the non-electric triggering system made of plastic tubing that transferred a shot of reactive chemicals that would ignite the explosives. With both Rostein and Sergeant James behind the shield, they attached each line to the chemical trigger, a circular box with a central red button.

"Fire in the hole! Fire in the hole!" the sergeant shouted and pressed the button.

Pushing down on the trigger immediately broke the seal around the contained chemicals. In fewer than ten seconds they detonated. The body wriggled and fell to the ground.

Immediately after, Rostein called out the same warning and pressed the button. And after ten seconds, another explosion, and then another. Quickly, Rostein withdrew each line from the triggers, and they all hustled towards the downed creature for the second step.

At most, they each had five minutes until it would regenerate. Madeline took out her kit, a plastic box containing the bio-wires and hand tools needed to disable the central nervous system. A holler drew her attention for a moment where one of the Oversight team shot down a Jelly that had appeared nearby. A sharp break of air followed by a loud moist *pop*. Much as she was startled and intrigued by it, she forced herself back to her task. She could not allow herself to be distracted by anything, even a firefight. She fixed her eyes on the gelatinous mass, hands steady as she made an inverted t-incision from the center then unfolded the flesh to reveal the complex matter inside. If not for the optic lenses, the thread-like innards would appear exactly alike. With them, she could see the pulsing ultraviolet plasma leading from certain threads to the brain stem.

She took the bio-wires and connected them to the neural threads carefully. A press of the trigger sent the necessary chemicals propelling up the threads, immediately liquidizing the central nervous system, leaving behind a lump of dead gelatin. She removed the wires and moved on to the next creature. This one was routine, the same as the other that she had just cleared. She stopped briefly to check the progress of her peers.

The sudden lull of the immediate chaos caused her to look up to the sky with the floating Mites just off her peripheral vision. She looked back. The rest of the Oversight team moved toward the Mites, setting charges in a line at the base. The creature who was once the woman Dubrovin remained on the ground alone. Madeline walked towards the body. She could only glance at what remained of the woman's face and was thankful when the sergeant called her over.

"BioTech should take care of that," Sergeant James said.

"*Should*," Rostein said. "It's too bad they're not here. Luckily, you have me."

The sergeant scoffed.

"Hey, I may have washed out, but I'm good enough. We have most of the equipment in the office or we'll borrow the rest. I'll radio BioTech and tell them. I'm sure they'll be happy to offload the work."

"We'll do it," Madeline said abruptly.

Rostein smiled widely and patted Madeline on the shoulder. Sergeant James grimaced.

"Good decision," Rostein said. "I'll collect the samples and let them know."

Rostein walked away. Sergeant James blinked hard and shook her head to pull herself away from the sight. She pulled back the layers of sleeves with an index finger and checked her watch.

"Better eat now while they're at it," she said, more to herself than to Madeline.

"You can eat with all this going on?" she asked, looking at the Oversight team fighting in the distance and at the body still on the ground. Even the thought of food made Madeline queasy.

"Can't fight on an empty stomach," Sergeant James said factually.

She called over to Goodway and used the radio to summon Rostein. Their work stopped. For a moment Madeline was transfixed on the fighting.

"Oy!" Rostein shouted, breaking Madeline's concentration.

When Madeline turned, the three were gathered around the UTAV in various states of eating. Rostein waved her over.

"You didn't bring anything?" Rostein asked once Madeline approached.

Madeline twisted her face in indignation. "There's no way I'm eating at a time like this." Gunshots drew her attention back to the battle.

Rostein pointed at her. "Ah, you think that *now*. Don't eat now and you won't eat all day."

Sergeant James, in the midst of eating from a packet of tuna with a plastic spoon, pushed a mouthful of food to the side of her cheek. "I'll get something for you."

The sergeant finished eating and crumpled up the remains of the packet and tossed it and the spoon on the ground. She walked to the passenger side of the UTAV and rummaged under the front seat. She presented Madeline with a vacuum sealed, opaque, desert brown plastic bag.

"What's this?" Madeline asked.

"Ready Meal," she answered.

Goodway responded with a guttural noise, as if a fly were caught in his throat.

"They aren't that bad," Sergeant James said.

"They aren't that good."

"You eat them for calories, not taste."

Madeline opened the bag on the perforated edge and glanced at the contents. More brown packets, a small bag of fruit candy, and a pack of white gum. There was nothing satisfying in it.

"Maybe later," she said.

Madeline returned to the vehicle. She put the meal packet near her seat. She stopped to watch the Oversight team. There were dead Mites on the dirt, and a clearer sky.

Muffled calls suddenly blared across the team's radios. Sergeant James answered. Soon, Madeline got a tap on her shoulder.

"Let's go," Sergeant James said.

Madeline acknowledged and followed the order. As she passed Rostein, she noticed her scraping dirt into a small plastic box that hung from her belt by a thick shoestring.

Madeline's body felt heavy. The adrenaline began to subside, her eyes drooped, and her muscles surrendered. She found a seat in the back, rested her head, and began to doze. The jolt of the vehicle turning woke her. In those hazy first moments, she thought of the mangled woman praying that she would not die, even as the creatures mauled her flesh. She blinked awake and, feeling wetness, wiped drool from her cheek. A quick glance placed her superiors in the front seats. She met eyes with Rostein who grinned and then glanced down at the plastic container on her lap. Inside, sitting atop a thin surface of dirt, a fuzzy six-legged creature crawled up one of the corners. As it crept about the container, it showed a fleshy yellow underside.

"What's that?" Madeline asked groggily. She curled her nose in disgust.

"A Hag Moth," Rostein answered without looking away from it. She watched it with focused admiration. "I thought it was a spider when I saw it wiggling. They are around the south. I've never seen one so far north up here. . ." she paused to hunch, pressing her face closer to the plastic where the insect's hairy appendages touched the sides, and stroking it with her fingertip.

Watching the Hag Moth creep around inside made Madeline's skin prickle. She shuddered at the thought of its fuzzy legs.

"Where are you going to keep this one?" asked Sergeant James.

"In my room."

"I thought we weren't supposed to keep animals," mentioned Madeline, remembering her pre-deployment briefing.

"*Animals,* not arthropods," Rostein clarified.

"Yeah, I've seen your room. I didn't think there was any space left."

"I'll just start keeping them in the shop," she joked.

"That's all I need the commander to see."

The unit commander, Madeline thought, *what was his name again?* She tried to remember it from the chain of command list she was given in training. He was responsible for the entire operations of Combat Oversight, including the Ordnance Corps.

"It'd be nice for him to come by for once," said Captain Green.

"Out of sight suits me," said the sergeant.

"What're you going to call this one?" Goodway asked with mild interest.

Rostein straightened back up, keeping the container steady in both hands, and rested the back of her head on the inside wall.

Fuzzy McFuzzface, Madeline thought jokingly.

"Ethel," she announced, then glanced over at Goodway, "Now I'll have to find another one to call Lucy."

Rostein then turned her sights to Madeline and stared at her for some time.

"*You* need a nickname," Rostein said.

Goodway groaned.

"What?" She shrugged her shoulders, lifting her arms and elbows as she did. The gesture looked to Madeline like she was holding two watermelons in her hands. "You're still butt-sore that I called you 'Gramps'."

Madeline stifled a laugh. He did not answer.

"What's your first name?" she asked.

"Madeline."

"We should call you. . .'Mad'." Rostein said, "Yeah." Her eyes brightened at the idea, "'Mad' Yazzie."

She could not help but smile at the moniker, derivative though it was. As a child, the nicknames given to her seemed to emphasize her youth to make her cute or appealing: Maddy, Cutie, Princess, Kid. Being called "Mad" suited her. It was a name earned and she enjoyed the respect that gleamed from their eyes.

Madeline removed her gear, bit by bit, and paused as she heard the sounds of buzzing and distant screams.

"Hear that?" Madeline asked.

They shook their heads or otherwise furrowed their brows. She listened, trying to pinpoint where the sound originated. It could be more Mites following them. She looked through the front windshield. She leaned to look through it, only to be glanced at curiously by the captain, who was driving. Outside the window was nothing but dirt and horizon.

Her legs spasmed from fatigue. She began to feel her stomach cramping from hunger. She would remember to bring food next time. The farther they drove, the more relaxed she became as she felt herself falling asleep again. Gradually, the sounds receded.

A hard push on her shoulder forced her awake. It was Rostein telling her they were almost back at the base. Madeline straightened her posture and rubbed her cheek where it was sore from resting on the seat. Goodway removed a black cylinder from one of his vest pockets. He pressed it to his lips, inhaled, and the end illuminated white.

He closed his eyes. He rested his head on the back of the chair with his arms crossed in front of his chest. After a few minutes, his head gradually fell sideways, but he managed to keep his nicotine stick still hanging between his lips. He reminded her of the archetypical seasoned soldier, numbed to the violence.

Madeline struggled with the scale of it all. The training seemed ridiculous in comparison to the reality she had just witnessed. Dissecting a Mite inside a sanitary room, with fail-safes and emergency contingencies, seemed now to her that she had been a child playing with clay. She had known the dangers in conception only, as if she were still that little girl staring at the Ashfall from behind protective glass. There was nothing here to protect her but herself and her troops. She had been focused on killing them, destroying as many as possible. It seemed simple. That was before seeing the damage they could inflict.

"What did you think?" Rostein asked.

"What?" Madeline replied, roused from her stupor.

"About your first day out here in the real world."

"It was a long one," she said.

Madeline thought of the adrenaline, the convulsing creatures, and she was proud of herself for remembering her training and using it in the field. At school, recalling facts for written tests had seemed impossible. Yet even though there was the danger of war, she had been able to fight and work with her team. There was a word that she heard her classmates used in school.

"Lit," she said.

Rostein laughed at her in the way that adults did when they thought they knew more than she did. It was the same laugh her math teacher gave when Madeline offered what she thought was the right answer but which, after demonstration, showed how wrong she had been.

"Something funny?" she asked defensively.

"Relax," Rostein said. "You did great for being so wet behind the ears. It'd be no fun if you blew yourself up on the first day."

5

Their convoy returned to the base after a thorough vehicle search. Upon returning to the shop, there was a brief discussion with Captain Green to summarize the day. She found it disheartening that, after hours in the vacant landscape where one misstep could result in maiming or death, she could divulge their day in a few quick sentences. Then came the tedious paperwork. They split the duties between them, with Rostein writing the official report as she instructed them on the procedural steps while periodically checking on the insect that sat in the container on her desk.

Rostein had coordinated all they needed to dispose of the remnants. What was left of the Mites were lifeless masses, their weight and texture not unlike the feel of a soft crustacean. Disposing of them required the liquid sealed within the yellow canister marked with a biohazard symbol. They wore protective smocks, gloves that rose to their elbows, goggles, a mask and unflattering skull caps. Madeline opened the round top, exposing the deceptively still, clear liquid. One could be forgiven in thinking it was water if it were not for the acrid smell and its destructive purpose. One by one, Goodway dropped the dead in and watched as they dissolved.

Madeline paused. They looked different in training.

"I thought it would've been bigger," she said.

"They make them smaller sometimes so that they can just wound us, incapacitate us, and try to change us into one of them," Goodway responded without looking.

Madeline could not find the words to respond to the grim fact. It was a reminder of the war in the most blatant way. Without it, it would seem as if what they did was the same training as always; training without consequence. It would have been easy for Madeline to revel in the similarities between training and war. She was eager to do her job and do it well.

Each Mite sizzled into a foamy film until the surface settled once more. Watching as her enemy completely disappeared, Madeline wondered briefly if the creatures had the same fear of death as humans.

Silly, she thought, *they were mindless.*

No more intelligent than the Mites they were named after. She remembered dissecting one in her training. Beneath the skin, there was only the most basic of bodily systems. An uncomplicated nervous system and the most miniscule of brains.

She studied them through reading research of their behavior. From her training she knew what comprised their physiology: Carbon based chromatophore fibers, muscles, a circulatory and nervous system. The prominent hypothesis was that they must have evolved in the ocean, a mysterious species kept hidden from humanity in the deepest oceanic depths until they emerged. They were alien, though they had not come from without, but within. From the oceanic abyss. Much research had been done on their biology, but their purpose beyond reproduction and assimilation remained unknown. And as she had seen with her own eyes, they were expanding their territory, however slowly.

"Done," Madeline said at the last disposal.

Rostein exhaled, blowing air from her mouth in a way that puffed her cheeks outwards, and finished writing. She pushed out her chair and stood up to stretch her arms out until her shoulders popped. Rostein made eye contact with Madeline.

"Took long enough," she said and grabbed the paperwork, walked into the sergeant's office, deposited it on his desk, and returned. She gently picked up the insect from her desk and held it in both hands.

"I'm out," she said, and left.

At the close of the door, Goodway scoffed.

"Shirking chain of command," he said.

She put her tools down and looked up to meet Goodway staring at her with an eyebrow raised.

"What?"

"Rostein," he clarified. "She's supposed to clear it with her squad lead before getting off."

Madeline clenched her jaw and took a deep breath.

"I'm too tired to deal with it," Madeline said truthfully. As a subordinate, Rostein should have asked permission. Had it been any other time, when she had more energy to handle interpersonal drama, she might have rushed to confrontation.

"Better to make them respect you early, or else."

"Or else, what?"

He made an open gesture with his arms. "Or else you end up like me."

"A grumpy old man?" she asked.

He pointed at her with a limp index finger.

"Exactly," he said.

Madeline could not decide whether or not to carry on the conversation. She did not have to. Goodway began to clean the area and she followed suit, both working in parallel silence until he asked if he could finish for the day. Once giving him permission, Goodway then left without a farewell. Soon Madeline did the same. After she dismissed herself from the office, a tightening of her belly drove her to find something savory and fresh from the dining hall.

Refreshed, Madeline checked the post office. It was an old portable, the kind she remembered using when she was in elementary school. Her boots clomped on the steps. There was a line inside. People rotated in and out carrying boxes or handfuls of letters. When it was her turn, she received a single, small package, wrapped in silver duct tape all around. She took it back to her room, fumbled with the wrapping and then eventually took a knife to it.

Sitting on the top was a letter. When she picked it up, she saw pictures underneath, and a black velvet pouch. She opened the pouch strings and upended the contents in her palm. It was silver inverted crescent Naja pendant on a silver chain. Normally, she was averse to jewelry of any kind, but this she fastened around her neck immediately. She tucked it under her shirt collar, so it settled next to her skin. She looked at the pictures; most of them were of the baby, though Eli could hardly be called a baby anymore. In the six months she had been gone at training, he'd grown. His face was fuller, which she was happy to see. In one, he was crawling on one of the cots, heading towards the camera with a large, open, drooling mouth and Fiona in the background looking on.

Madeline opened the envelope. Inside was the letter, written on a plain white paper atop. It took her some time to decipher the writing, which changed a few paragraphs in, and then again, noting that each family member had a turn to write a note. The first was her sister, thanking her for the money. As soon as Madeline received her signing bonus, she made sure to set up an allotment transferring the better part of her pay directly to her parents. They were able to buy food for Eli, and extras to share. They hoped to save money to move into a cheap apartment.

She returned the letter to the envelope and placed it gingerly onto the bedside table. She was satisfied that they were doing well. She felt like an adult: responsible, powerful, and making a difference.

She peeled off her uniform and left each piece where it fell on the ground. Madeline went to the bathroom where there stood a short stand up shower, a toilet, and a sink. Turning the silver faucet on, a shower of hot water shot out from the spout to create a low steam. She stepped into the welcome heat of the water as it spilled over her face and shoulders. At times she would turn away to let it stream down her back, then she would open her mouth and breathe in the clean fumes that rose from the steam. Luxuriating in the waterfall created the guilt of indulgence. While a refugee, she and her family often had to wait in line for water rations and every drop was precious.

Madeline wobbled. She blinked to keep awake. Shutting the water off, she patted dry, and returned to the main room. She wore one of her clean uniform undershirts and slipped on the cozy socks from her sister. The mattress was still bare, but she was too tired to worry about sheets. She turned on the small television. The channels were mostly static, except for a few military transmissions of popular television shows. The channel cut out frequently, making the attempt at watching pointless. She turned on her side, to the only window in her room, and looked at the twinkling stars as she felt herself falling asleep. She should take out her optic lenses. Leaving them in too long had affects. But she could not lift her heavy arms. Eyelids drooped involuntarily. In the back of her mind were whispers and the blurry image of an eviscerated woman.

6

The next morning began with a phone call from Sergeant James. There was an early call from an Oversight team.

"Command wants us to double the route clearance today," she said, accompanied with an irritated sigh, "You and your team will follow along and then we'll split off. Be at the convoy in an hour."

Sergeant James hung up before Madeline could protest. She forced herself up and prepared for the day. Her uniform from the day before lay on the ground in a heap. She had two more clean ones and rustled through her bag to retrieve one.

At her arrival, Sergeant James hurried her over to an extra UTAV vehicle and pulled out a map while summarizing their mission. There were roads in a field, indiscriminate from one another except for small longitude and latitude marks. Madeline and her team would follow the convoy until a certain point, then remain with an Oversight team to clear the road. The captain and the sergeant had been given a separate task from the unit commander that Sergeant James explained as "secret for the sake of being secret."

"Stay in communication," Sergeant said. She folded the map once more and joined the captain in another vehicle.

With her troops and the other teams arriving, Madeline let Goodway drive the UTAV. They separated from the others since their road led them to the basin of a vertical hill scattered with shrubs. When they arrived, there were several Oversight soldiers waiting for them. Madeline dismounted from the UTAV. One of the soldiers ran up to them as Rostein and Goodway retrieved their tools.

"Took you all long enough," he said. "We found a few in there. They're probably not active, but you guys should take a look anyway."

Madeline looked up the steep hill to an alcove that was no taller than half of her height.

"Not active, huh?"

"I'm pretty sure. I could tell by looking at it."

"I really doubt it," she countered. "You can barely see Mites with just your eyes. You need these," she said, pointing an index finger at the edge of her right eye to draw attention to her specialized optic lenses.

"Whatever," the soldier said, "just deal with it."

He left to rejoin the other Oversight troops and she heard distant laughter from them that she chose to ignore.

"Should we check it out?" Rostein asked. "We don't usually do caves."

"Try the robot," Goodway suggested.

Madeline looked up to where the cave stood and glanced back at the vehicle.

"Maybe it would work this time," Goodway added.

"Yeah, but we can't bust the sensors," Rostein said. "Those things are finicky."

"Not to mention expensive," Goodway added.

So many rules, Madeline thought.

"So, we'll all carry it up," Madeline groaned.

Rostein pursed her lips. "It could work. We'll have to keep it steady."

Madeline jumped down to where Goodway and Rostein were propping up the robot. She looked at them.

"Let's get it up there."

They each stood at one side of the robot to form a triangle. Madeline squatted down and counted off to three so that they all lifted simultaneously. Though the robot was light with the three lifting it, they stepped solidly against the surface to avoid dropping the sensitive instrumentation in their hands. At times, their feet would slip, causing rocks to fall down the slope behind them as they managed to lift the robot to the cave and settle it on the flat surface a few inches inside. They left the robot there and descended.

"Rostein, you can get on the controls."

"Right," she acknowledged.

Rostein approached the inside of the UTAV where a set of four screens had been set up that reflected what the robot cameras saw. Below it was a set of controls, including a joystick that she tapped sensitively to move the robot forward. Madeline and Goodway hunched so they could gaze over Rostein's shoulder as she guided the robot through the cave.

"Nice job," Goodway said.

Rostein gave a sideways grin. "You've never seen me play video games, have you? That's even more impressive."

"Really? What games?"

"Oh, you can watch me play whenever we get out of this. I'm a beast when it comes to gaming."

Madeline watched the screen intently, waiting for some sign and hoping that she could see something.

"Shooters?"

"Nah. Those are for noobs. I only play the hard games, the really brain-busting ones that would make you rage-quit." Rostein paused. "Hello Kitty's Island Adventure."

Both Goodway and Madeline laughed.

"I think there's something over there," Rostein said. Their laughter faded as Rostein pointed at the screen to an area just beyond some rocks. She stopped the robot.

They watched it come to a cache of immature Mites all stacked upon each other delicately.

"Babies?" Rostein asked.

Madeline chuckled at the choice of the humanizing word. "Not what I'd call them."

"Can't be." Goodway blurted. "They don't reproduce this far out of their cluster."

"Well, they're here. Move in closer." Madeline suggested.

Rostein tapped the joystick forward as the camera moved along through the corridor. Simultaneously, the camera screens went blank and there was the low drone as the electronics were shutting down.

Madeline let out a slow, exasperated breath. "Well, there goes that robot."

She turned to Rostein and Goodway and said, "I'll check it out."

Rostein muttered something, which Madeline only heard "There goes Mad..."

Madeline took a shovel from the side locker of the UTAV and trudged back up the slope to the cave. There was the robot, stationary, and the cache some feet ahead of it.

Quivering masses.

Not eggs, she thought, *not quite.*

They were translucent fleshy tumors covering the ground, stuck to portions of the walls. Inside were countless dark eyes all squished together, pummeling for space. The closest she had seen them before was isolated, on a dissecting table, and in training simulations. It did not prepare her for seeing them up close.

They seemed to *breathe*.

Madeline would have to hurry. An egg colony meant that there would be others nearby. She pressed on her communication pin.

"Visual, copy," she whispered.

There was no response.

Of course, there wouldn't be, she thought, shaking her head at her temporary thoughtlessness. Even the eggs disrupted their technology.

Footsteps soon followed, and she turned to see the rest of her squad enter the cave.

"Shit," said Goodway, "let's get the thing and get out of here."

"Better to just leave it. Write it off," Rostein contradicted.

"What does the sergeant say?"

"Comms are shot," Madeline said.

"That's right," Rostein said, looking at Madeline, "Then it's your call."

Madeline had to think. She had to recover the robot. They might need it for later reconnaissance. Losing it would be a mistake. There was also the amount of eggs they found. Eggs meant more Mites. A better option mingled in her mind.

"I'll get the bot."

"You'll break something on it by taking it down by yourself," Rostein warned.

"Better off broken than lost, right?" Madeline added. So while I'm doing that, you both lay down controlled detonation around the area." Goodway smiled at the suggestion. "When we're back at the UTAV, we blow it."

"And run like hell," Rostein added with a wide grin.

Madeline looked at each of them to gauge their comfort. They would have to do it. She wouldn't linger on the possible heinous outcomes.

"Should we take any back with us? " Goodway asked, pointing at a nearby egg.

Madeline shook her head once, "Not our job."

"Let BioTech worry about research. It takes skills that *none* of us have to extract them."

"Speak for yourself," Goodway added.

"I *am*. I know enough from washing out of BioTech and landing here."

Goodway fell silent.

"Let's just get going," Madeline said.

It took longer than she expected for her to recover the robot, owing to how delicately she had to maneuver around the cache. Periodically, she checked with her troops as they lay charges. The detonators were arranged some feet from the cave entrance following a path to the center clusters. The membranes appeared fragile, yet Madeline recalled vaguely from her schooling that they were as a carapace, impenetrable but for the strongest explosives.

She moved with cautious expediency and was able to remove it from the stone covered cave. She tossed the shovel down the hillside and picked up the machine with both hands to descend the slope once more. She replaced the damaged robot within the UTAV and went back to pick up her shovel.

Madeline felt the twinges of fatigue. She had to keep blinking to focus her attention. Her body would have to comply. She found the red spool that held the charging wire and she rushed back up the hill. Goodway and Rostein continued attaching lines to the detonators.

"Almost through?" she asked.

Their faces were flushed from the heat within the cave.

"Three more," Rostein said.

Madeline held out her open hand. "Give me some. We gotta move."

Rostein handed her some charges.

Madeline found an egg cluster on the slant of the cave. She placed the charge on the top. Drawn to the heart, the squiggling eyes turned to it. The cluster's large eyes under the slim flesh and squishy body made it look like a pleading tadpole.

"Don't look at me," she murmured to the creature.

Even as she was determined not to look at it, her peripheral vision wandered towards their movements.

They'll grow more, she thought. *Better to just get rid of them now before that can happen.*

She finished securing the wires, then threaded them gently towards the detonator. Madeline waited there for Goodway and Rostein, who hunched over, repeating the same action as she had done a few moments before. When they had finished, Madeline checked that each wire was properly affixed to the detonator charges. She took the red spool and attached one end of the charging wire to the detonator input.

Satisfied, she said, "Let's go."

They descended the outside hill as Madeline gently pulled the charging wire with her, laying it in a thread down the hillside while Rostein and Goodway hopped into the vehicle with the detonator in hand. When she was at the bottom of the hill, Madeline cut the wire off the spool and handed it to Rostein who attached it to the detonator.

Madeline entered the driver's side. A fresh wave of excitement came from being behind the wheel. She had not driven a UTAV since training. She started the vehicle and kept her boot hovering over the acceleration pad. She checked her watch for the time.

"Okay. Light it up," Madeline said.

Rostein pressed the button. The explosions were immediate. It was as if the cave entrance vomited dirt and debris and bits of carapace. Rostein removed the wire and dropped it to the ground. Madeline kept watch on the rearview mirror as the debris cloud reached closer. In the distance, a dark shape emerged. It was the shape and stature of a giant cuttlefish, larger than a blue whale, eyeless, with its apex pointed downwards and its tendrils gathered above it. A Damocles Spear.

"Yazzie!" Goodway shouted in alarm.

"I see it."

Madeline pressed her foot down on the accelerator.

The sky turned a grim violet. It loomed in the near distance, facing their direction. Its tentacles fanned outward. Its skin changed, becoming covered in glowing azure spots. Madeline drove as quickly as the vehicle allowed, speeding over the naked plains, as she checked the rear-view mirror to see the darkness there, ever present, unrelenting. She murmured to herself, trying to will the creature away. Damocles Spears did not usually follow for long. The vehicle slowed, refusing to adhere to Madeline's stubborn pressing of the pedal. In response, Rostein readied her weapon.

They were all quiet, ready for what might come next. The vehicle slowed, losing any momentum, until it stopped completely. Madeline cursed. She held her hand on the door handle and opened it just enough so she could peek out. It was there, like a storm cloud on the horizon. Madeline was tempted to raise her weapon and fire.

"You think I could pick it off?" she asked.

Goodway scoffed.

"You'd be the first one to do it," Rostein added. "There's a reason we don't engage these ones unless we have to. We're not infantry."

"*Your* gun is up," Madeline countered.

"Just in case," she said. "But it'd be nice if we got through today without another incident. Blowing up those eggs maxed me out of my adrenaline."

Madeline paused. Much as she might want to attack the creature, she realized that she already risked all their lives today and managed to survive. Provoking further action would not be fair to her troops. Madeline closed the door. The best course of action would be to do nothing and hope the creature passed without incident. Though they had some protection by remaining inside the vehicle, should the Damocles Spear choose to release its Ash, there was little to stop it from filtering through the cracks and infesting their skin.

None of them spoke. They waited in silence as the violet sky consumed them. A sound like the low melody of crooning whales came from above. The vehicle rattled with the vibrations. Madeline reached into her blouse to touch the pendant that hung from the chain around her neck.

Light flushed back through the windows. As soon as the creature had come, it was gone. There was a collective relief. The clacking of weapons lowering, the sigh of bodies relaxing, meant they were free from immediate danger. Madeline opened the door again, peered out, and watched as the Damocles Spear flowed away on the currents under the clouds. With the creature leaving, she shut the door and tried the accelerator again. The vehicle sprung to life.

The closer they came to base, the more Madeline was relieved. She watched out the window with her left elbow resting on the lip and her fingers tapping gently against the glass. She shifted her eyes over the passing scenery.

"I wish the weather would clear up," Rostein said.

"You'd rather have hundred-degree heat?" Goodway asked. "I'll take *this*. Mites move slower in the cold."

"That's a myth," Madeline said, remembering her training.

Once they returned to the shop, Rostein got out of the vehicle first.

"Let's see how messed up that bot is," she said. A few minutes later, loud cursing emanated from out of sight and there was a distinct slam of the shop door closing. Goodway glanced at Madeline, sighed, and went inside, which left Madeline alone to take the remains of the robot inside and place it on the wooden floor.

At the sound of the noise, Captain Green came out of his office.

"I heard the call come through," he said as he stood up from his desk to assess the robot. When he saw it, he groaned, exasperated. He bent over to hold his face closer to the mangled steel skeleton.

"It tripped the cache or something. It looked like it had been there awhile anyway. We'll see if we can fix it up." Madeline said, trying to explain to temper his disappointment.

Captain Green nodded.

"You'll have to fix it up. We can't write it off," he said. "Declaring it out of service will get the commander busting through the door. You know how much those cost?"

"Yeah," she said. "I'll get to it."

"Hold up--"

Madeline paused.

"There's also the problem of you blowing the cache."

Madeline scrunched her face in confusion. "What? How is that a problem?"

"What are your operating procedures?"

She sighed. "I called. Comms weren't working."

"And you could have returned to a range where they *would* work."

"I--" she had not thought of that. "I thought getting rid of them was more important."

"More important than your troops' lives? Than yours? You *should* have established the location and returned to report it." It was a lecture, but his emotion never showed except for the lowering of his voice, "Did you even consider that there might be another use for a cache like that?"

There was no answer for him. She looked at the captain, lips pressed together, stubborn.

"I thought I did the right thing."

His reaction to that was a downturn of his lips that revealed deep lines around his mouth. He opened his desk drawer and heaved a tattered paperback book onto the piles of paperwork atop his desk. The cover was almost completely worn which made the title barely readable. The edges were fuzzy, and there was a clear tear from the top to a few inches down the center that had been duct taped together.

"Read, study, and *attempt* some critical thinking," he said. "Ordnance is about using your brain. If you want to fight like a grunt, I have no problem putting you in for job reclassification."

"No," she said. Foot soldiers were paid less and died more often. "I'll--I'm sorry, I'll do better," she offered.

"Don't be sorry; be useful." The captain said. "Repair the bot as best as you can. Dismissed."

Madeline wanted to say more to defend herself, to apologize, to explain. But when an officer gave an order, she knew she had to abide. She pressed her lips together, took the book that was small enough to fit in her pants pocket, and left.

7

Goodway and Rostein gathered the spare equipment, tools, and repair manual while Madeline removed her helmet and vest and left them in a pile on the floor. Without them on, her body felt lighter than usual. They worked together for hours into the evening in an attempt to repair the remains of the robot, to salvage the equipment that cost well over four hundred thousand dollars. She spouted off lines of curses when her tool would slip and took smoke breaks to keep the time moving. She had not realized until she looked at her watch that the light outside grew darker and both Rostein and Goodway's attentions were fading quickly. She stretched her shoulders back until they popped and looked at the weary faces of her team.

"You guys can go back to your rooms. I'll try to finish up here."

Rostein perked up. "Are you sure?".

Madeline nodded and saw her soon depart from the shop. Goodway straightened his back. Madeline dove back into the repairs. She looked at the contents of the open control panel. Electrical wires poked out. Some were tangled and others had burn marks. Repairing the damage would be impossible. They should be replaced, but the replacement wires in her supply case were sized differently, incompatible with the robot.

"Whoever ordered these supplies was an idiot," she murmured. "I thought the military was supposed to have the best of everything."

Goodway chuckled.

"In some golden age, maybe. You get some good stuff: The UTAV, the kits, and then you get some of the Oversight guys who wear plastic helmets under that camo because Defense didn't want to spend more than they had to on steel."

"That can't be right."

"Yeah? Go ask them to show their helmet next time we roll out."

She scratched off the wire casing to expose the naked wires. She removed the main line wire to replace them with the twisted wires. These she inserted into the circuitry and secured them with electrical tape. She switched it on. When nothing happened, she pinched the wires. A short electrical current sent a mild shock through her fingers. She let out a victorious laugh.

She picked up the remote, pushed the joystick and the robot twitched. She moved it again, with no result. At a point she stopped and stepped back from the table and stared at it with her arms crossed. She needed a break and went outside. When she did, she saw Rostein some distance away, walking in slow, determined steps, then she stopped to crouch in an attempt to snatch night bugs with her hands.

Madeline felt dizzy. Her legs threatened to give way, so she sat down on the dirty ground. Her chest tightened. It was as if she had a rock wedged in her ribcage. She tilted her head upwards to open her throat to more air. The moon hung as a crescent in the starry night where not a cloud obstructed its scene. She could recognize some of the stars.

"Madeline," she remembered her mother's voice.

She would point to the night sky and connect them together with her fingertip. Her father might be there. Fiona will have already been asleep.

"That's Orion," she marked.

She drew her finger over the midsection.

"But there--" she pointed to another section of the darkness above "--that is the Big Dipper."

She again traced it with her finger along the dots in such a way as to outline the image of a cup attached to a handle. When she lifted her arm up, her silver and turquoise bracelets jingled together against her wrists.

"And once you find that one, then the little one isn't far behind." she said with a sweet grin.

"Let's see if you can find it."

"Me?" she asked.

"Go on," she encouraged.

Her juvenile eyes turned up to the sky and desperately tried to find the spot where the Big Dipper was that she had traced not a few minutes before.

"It's easiest to find the bright star that hangs on the tip of the dipper." she offered.

Madeline searched for the bright star but failed to see it among all of the millions of others that sparkled.

"I can't find it," she grumbled.

"Don't worry. Here--" she took her hand and lifted it up, "point." she instructed. Madeline did so. With her finger she moved her arm to the spot where the Dubhe star shone and put her finger to it.

"You see? That's where it starts, and then you can see the rest of the dipper."

She guided her hand so that her own finger traced the boundaries of the constellation.

"You see?" she asked cheerfully.

"And from there," she moved her wrist down to a point and settled on a brighter, fuller star, "*that* is the North Star."

With her eyes to the sky, she found the seven stars that etched the lines of the Big Dipper and followed their direction to the brightest pearl in the sky. It brought her some small comfort that the ancient stars that plague the sky stood barely unchanged for a millennium. Whatever happened where she stood on the ground, whether she lived or died, whether humanity lived or died, the stars would remain. Some things were, at least, barely changeable. A single star lasted millions of years, staring down at the pitiful beings of the Earth. How brightly would they shine when all the humans of the world had been stamped out by time? With none to look upon them save beasts and Mites.

"What are you looking at?" Goodway asked.

Madeline turned her head down to see him as she inhaled from his cigarette, then tossed it on the ground and stamped it with his boot while exhaling the smoke out of his mouth.

"The stars," she answered without inflection.

If he thought it was a strange answer, then he did not show it. He looked up to where she gazed, then scratched his neck.

"This thing has been irritating me," he said. Goodway fiddled with the chain around his neck, then from out of his shirt he pulled at the chain from which his dog tags hung. Clinking against them was a small charm.

"What is it?" Madeline asked.

She pointed to the trinket on the chain. The shape was obscured by the darkness, and she could only decipher the glint of silver.

Reflexively, he touched it. "Jerusalem Cross." He smiled. "Every little bit helps."

God willing, she thought reflexively.

She hadn't thought like that since the Ashfall. After that, there were so many prayers. There was only so much she could remember about the madness that followed the creatures' descent upon her home. Confusion, disassociation, denial of reality. When she thought of it, it was as if she were experiencing it through a stranger's eyes as she watched her younger self following her parent's frantic instructions. Who was that girl? She joined thousands of others. Different colored faces with the same bewildered, unblinking, expression. The same question painted onto each face, seeming to ask "Why?" or "How?" She wondered whether the answer would make any difference.

Goodway eyed her, furrowing his brows.

She shook her head. "No. I don't follow any of that," she kicked at the dirt absentmindedly. A pebble came loose, and she rolled it under her boot heel.

"Some things just stick," Goodway said.

Madeline nodded. There had to be some kind of justice. If they could all be destroyed, then what happened to her would not happen to anyone else. Again, the eviscerated woman appeared, and with her, the buzzing.

"How--" Madeline started but wrestled with whether to broach the subject or to ignore it, and then decided on the former, "How do you deal with the dying?"

He looked at her with an expression that seemed to Madeline like pity.

"Do you want one?" he asked as he took out a lighter to inflame the cigarette now nestled between his teeth. She thought for a moment, unsure. In school, she remembered posters that warned against smoking, even as she snuck outside before homeroom once to try a cigarette with Juniper. When she got home, her mother smelled it on her. She tried off and on to quit and considered refusing Goodway. But, then again, why not? What did she have to lose? Smoking would not cause cancer for decades. She could die tomorrow.

"Yes." she said. "If I can go to war, I can smoke."

He held out the pack and the lighter towards her. She took one cigarette and lit it against the flame. She inhaled too strongly. She coughed, retched, and spat out the taste. Goodway laughed. She tried again, this time slowly, remembering how she saw Juniper smoke that day, and how actors smoked in movies. She coughed again, but did not choke, and sputtered out the smoke.

"Dying happens and you move on," he said finally. "There's nothing much we can do about that."

"Yeah," she thought of the day the Ash fell from the sky and the dead on the ground. She conceded, "I guess not."

"Why'd you join?" he asked.

She recalled a starving baby's cry and the vision of the Damocles Spear.

"Because it was the fastest way to get money." she looked at the burning end of the cigarette. "And I wanted to light up as many of them as I could."

He nodded once and looked at her with a platonic affection.

"I can't blame you for that."

"What about you?" Madeline asked.

He smiled. "Bad luck."

He tossed the cigarette on the ground, stamped it out, and lit another one. Madeline took another draw, more confident this time, and when she exhaled, felt a soft numbness permeated her entire body. She relaxed. She did not realize how tense she had been until relaxation set in.

"I've been in for eight years. Back when we were killing each *other* instead of *them*. I didn't know they started automatic re-enlistments, so I've been stuck. I had a pretty skate comm job, but they pulled me and re-trained me through the Ordnance Corps."

Madeline paused. "They make you stay in?"

"Unless you do the paperwork to *de*-enlist, and then pop that bug out your arm, yeah; Quitting's not an option."

She thought about the tiny global positioning tracking capsule the recruiter implanted just under the skin on her left shoulder. The knowledge made her groan. Absence of choice left bitterness in her throat. She would have to endure it for the greater cause.

"You don't sound like you want to be here," Madeline said with a hint of judgment.

He chuckled. "No sane person does, Mad. If they gave me my discharge papers tonight, I'd take them."

"But we have to get rid of them," she said.

"Can any of us do that?" he queried. "If nukes didn't kill them, what will? Throwing thousands of us against them, hoping we'll do enough damage?" He shook his head.

"We can try," Madeline said.

Goodway exhaled. "I'll just do my job."

She took a draw. The gargantuan Damocles Spear and the phosphorescent sky that was gradually, unendingly, consuming their own was all she could think about.

"Do you think we can actually win?" she asked. She had not wanted to admit it out loud to anyone, even to herself that she had doubts.

He shrugged, shook his head, scratched the back of his left earlobe.

"Who knows?" He tossed the cigarette on the dirt, stamped it out with the tip of his boot and then lit another cigarette. "I wasn't sure about you," he admitted, "We're the same rank, sure, but you're technically my superior since you volunteered. I didn't want to be bossed around by an upstart teenager, but I think you're alright. Busting up that cache today took gumption."

Madeline beamed with the sense of earned respect.

"Captain didn't think so," she said.

"Ah, well. He wasn't there, was he?"

She reached into her pocket and pulled out the book.

"He gave me this to study."

"Hey!" he exclaimed, "I haven't seen one of these since I was in basic." He took it from her and opened it to a random page. "It's an old field manual," he said, holding it closely to his face to read in the darkness. He closed it and handed it back. Madeline took it and returned the book to her pocket.

"There's some good stuff in it," Goodway said, "my first deployment we had a vehicle end up in a ditch and had to figure out how to tow it out. First time using a trucker's hitch," he said.

Madeline looked over at the sky that was turning into a haze of orange and purple. There was a chill breeze that passed by the two of them. Madeline shivered. The dauntlessness from earlier that day faded with the light. She decided to trust Goodway with her doubt.

"I feel like I don't know what I'm doing," she confessed.

She expected admonishment from the older man. Instead, he said, "We all do the best we can. Mites take everything. Have you seen any animals since we've been here?"

At his mention of it, she remembered her training modules that detailed what was known about the Helgrammaw, and then the multiple-choice tests afterwards. It had stuck at the time, but it was hard to remember it all now; it had leaked out somewhere. All the reading, the staring at screens, the cramming, testing, and then forgetting it all so that she could go through the next round of reading, staring at screens, and then cramming. She remembered some of it, that the creatures changed the mammalian, the reptilian, but not insects.

"No," she answered.

"They're coming for all of us, in the end." He flicked the end of his cigarette on the ground. "Why did you decide to go for this?" he asked.

"Lots of reasons," she answered vaguely at first, not wanting to share her personal affairs. While looking at the cigarette between her fingers, she reconsidered. "There was a baby, my sister's baby, and we were stuck in a refugee center. I thought it was a good chance for me to *do* something."

He nodded in understanding. Like her, most joined after the creatures appeared either due to the desire for vengeance, the need to assist humanity, or of necessity. The Ashfall had made refugees of millions and military recruiters took the opportunity to offer them stability in the form of salary, shelter, and food, despite the personal risks.

She shrugged, tossed her cigarette to the ground, and stamped it out.

"Have a good night," he said.

As he walked away, he periodically stopped to look at the stones on the ground. Madeline reflected on his departure, and the conversations she had since her boots touched dirt. They had, for the most part, been curt. It was the same while she was in training. No time wasted talking. If there were a lull, it was spent catching sleep or talking about nothing, in much the same way as she had done amongst her friends in school.

She looked up to the sky once more where the stars gleamed dimmer until they were obscured by a gently moving cloud. Madeline blinked again to refresh her vision. It was not a cloud.

The alarm sounded. It caused the same robust excitement as when she heard it that day in school. Alarm Code Red. The loud voice on the speakers told them to shelter-in-place. Do not engage.

The creatures were coming, and they would be close. Madeline wanted to retrieve her weapon, her ordnance kit, and go after them. Kill as many as she could. That was "Mad" thinking. She thought of the sergeant, the egg cache, and the orders sounding from the giant voice. Madeline had never been told or heard of Mites wandering so close to their bases. If they assimilated by ground, it happened with their floating Ash first, and a Damocles Spear, with the Mites appearing later. What she knew of them was as a hive-mind, following commands unquestioningly. If they were here, it was because they were told to be. A horrible realization erupted from deep within the forefront of her mind. They were here because of what Madeline did to the eggs.

She should do something. Get a knife and stab any of them that get close. She thought of the woman, the entangled woman. Too close and they would wrap their tendrils around any part of her skin and that would be the end of her story. She would not let that happen. Not so soon. She would remain a bystander, much to her frustration. What she remembered of her training modules in the event of this exact situation told her to retreat to the nearest building. That would have been to go back inside the flight building. She preferred not to spend an uncountable amount of time in what she expected to be a crowded, uncomfortable space. She instead diverted to her room, hoping she was not seen.

When Madeline returned to her room, she shut and locked the door. As if locking it would stop them. It was a reflexive gesture, subconscious, an act born out of needing control. She paced, turned on the television, found it static, turned it off again, then went to the window. In the darkness they were there, seen only by the disappearing stars. Shadows appeared along the fence line. Then came colorful lights in the night. If she could forget, just for a moment, it could have been beautiful. The landscape was dotted with sparse trees that were covered in frost. She imagined how they would look dressed up like Christmas trees in the distance and admired how similar it looked to the winter plains at home when the air seemed to crystallize, and the sky was so close it was as if she could leap and swim into the clear pool.

Madeline turned from the window and opened the drawer, taking the old book where she had stored the letter from her family and read it once more.

I should write back, she thought.

After seeing the Damocles Spear, she wanted to write something to them in case the worst happened. Having no decent paper, she used her field notebook and pen. Writing her thoughts and feelings was never a strong suit. In her school English class, she could barely etch out a paragraph of free writing, let alone an essay, then became frustrated in looking around the room to see her classmates, or her friend, Juniper, moving their pencils across the page with ease. How quaint to think of it. Her old frustrations paled in comparison to the gravity of the war around her and those classmates and friends that she knew were gone.

Madeline wrote as much as she could, three pages worth, pouring her feelings, her mistakes, her frustrations.

The training should have been good enough, she thought, remembering the hours upon hours that she spent during her technical training practicing simulations and trial after trial of mock controlled detonations. The course had been rigorous with an eighty percent attrition rate to ensure that only the most capable could serve in the Ordnance Corps. Even so, it was two weeks. At the time it seemed like long enough to Madeline.

Maybe it's not just the training, Madeline considered. *Maybe I need to change. Training was one thing but that's not enough for this place. I have to be different.*

Finishing the letter, she placed the pages in the book. She was about to close the cover when on the following book page, she stopped a moment to read:

But on you will go, though the weather be foul
On you will go, though your enemies prowl.

Madeline closed the children's book, placed it safely in her drawer, took out the field manual, opened it to the first page, and began reading.

8

adeline took off her armored vest with a quick tug of the straps and a swift pull over her head. Though she had become accustomed to the weight, it was still a relief to remove it. She breathed deeply, gathering a full unhindered inhale. She pulled off her boots, bombarded immediately by a stench akin to rotting cotton. Her socks were soaked with sweat from the summer heat. She removed them to stuff them in her boots, careful to hold her breath, then threw her boots into the corner of her room, distancing them as far from her person as possible. Madeline scratched an itch on the back of her neck and felt a welt there. With the heat came mosquitos, thousands of them. They were breeding exponentially with their natural predators removed.

Madeline reached into her breast pocket to retrieve a crumpled pack of cigarettes and a lighter. She immediately found comfort in the cigarette between her lips, the fire inflaming the end. She replaced the pack and lighter and reclined onto her bed. The rank sweat from the day stuck to her skin, creating a film. She sped through the cigarette, extinguished it in an empty can of Amp Energy on her bedside table, and wiped a sheen of sweat from the back of her neck. The creatures were getting faster. More erupted each day. They could hardly count them all at a glance. The heat made them quicken. It was exhausting work to beat back their offspring.

Madeline sat on her bed which she had finally furnished with standard white bed sheets and reached over into her bedside drawer. She pulled out a handheld electric fan. She placed it in front of her face and flipped the plastic switch. The fan whirred in her face, blowing lukewarm air. It was enough to cool her down and ease her into sleep. She clicked off the fan and dropped it onto the floor.

On these days, she missed her family the most. They may as well be a world away in the south where a humid veil covered everything, and the heat was relentless. It stuck to her skin, covering her like a steamy wet blanket. When it became too much, her mother would lie her down in the shade and fan her face, giving her temporary reprieve. More often than not, they would sit in silence, but on occasion her mother would hum. If her sister were lucky, she would bring back ice from the canteen and they would all stroke the cool cubes on their foreheads. When she closed her eyes, she could hear her mother humming and the gentle swishing of a fan.

The novelty of her situation rapidly wore through her optimism. There was a routine to it. Each day blended into the next, intermittent sleep between them, and a day or two mixed in where she might recuperate. Each day, she and her team destroyed as many Mites as they could, trying to push them back. And each day, more spawned. She came to query if it was an impossible task, like trying to bail a sinking boat with a sieve. Still, she decided that it was better to do something than nothing at all.

A telephone ring roused her from a fatigued sleep. Sluggishly, she picked up the receiver, eyes half-closed.

"Oversight is going out in three hours," Captain Green said. "New route, so I'll be out with you."

"Copy," she grumbled.

"Try to get some more sleep and I'll meet you there."

She had to call Rostein and Goodway next. They answered similarly to the way she did; agitated, but compliant.

She set an alarm and then woke what seemed like only seconds after. Slightly better rested, she took a brief shower to rinse off the dry sweat, then placed her optic lenses in and dressed in a clean uniform. She made sure to grab her backpack full of pre-packaged meals and water. On her way out, she breezed past her troops' door, knocking until they woke to ensure that they were up and ready. Her walk to the meeting point ensured that she passed the Amp Energy vending machine. There were two people in front of her. The one in front kept scanning his card over the magnetic reader. Cans tumbled out, one after the other that he would then stuff into his backpack. She worried that he would buy them all and she needed them. She decided to ask the man in front of her if he would not mind moving. Otherwise, she would have to find another vending machine. She tapped the man in front of her on the shoulder.

"Let me go next?" she asked.

He glanced at her and then looked again, more scrutinous the second time.

"Crawl back to your mom to wipe that snot off your nose," he said with a self-satisfied grin.

Madeline had no patience for him and noted his lower rank. As a rule, she had not used her rank to shuffle through minor annoyances. Yet, she was an Engineer, she was "Mad". She had authority among her squadron, and she could not shoulder this man's disrespect.

"You'd better check yourself," she said, and tapped her higher rank with her finger. He noticed, rolled his eyes, and reluctantly stepped back. Madeline had her turn, bought three of the cans, and left.

When she met up with the convoy, it was just her, the captain, and a few Oversight troops who were putting on their gear. Madeline remembered what Goodway said before about their cheap helmets. She approached one of the men. His name tape was obscured by his hand as he shrugged his armored vest over one shoulder. He was a young man she guessed was close to her own age, clean shaven, with what looked like acne on the right side of his face. His expression was wary as she approached, and he tried to avoid making eye contact.

"Hey," she started.

When he finished putting on his vest, she noted his name and rank.

"Can I check out your helmet?" she asked.

He shrugged, reached for a round canister from his side pants pocket, and with the other, released the strap and handed her the helmet. She took it, all the while curious as to what he was doing with the tin. He opened the top. Inside the contents was a moist brown substance that looked to her like tar. He pinched some with a thumb and forefinger, pressed it between his gum and lip, closed the tin, and replaced it in his pocket. Madeline looked back down at the helmet, tapped it with her knuckle. It made a hollow sound. She pulled the fabric lining to check the inner armor.

"Are you 'Mad'?" he asked.

"That's what they call me," she said, her eyes fixed on the helmet.

"Yeah, well don't go doing anything crazy. It's us that have to back you all up. If you go running off, it's our asses that have to cover *you*."

Madeline was insulted by his immediate judgment. Ordnance was important. She and her comrades could completely destroy the creatures. The Oversight could only slow them down. If robots were not made impotent by the Helgrammaw, there would be no need for additional lives to risk. It was also not her fault, she considered, that the troops were their protection. She might have said this all but was too tired to spend the mental energy debating him. All she said was, "I'd just go by myself if it were up to me."

She managed to separate the lining. What she saw made her mouth open slightly, as if to ask "Why?" but then remained frozen, because she knew the answer. Goodway had been correct. Under the camouflage was not the hardened metal that should protect a human life, but a hard-black plastic shell.

"You're crazier than I am if you wear this," she said as she gave it back. "What's the point?"

He strapped it back on.

"It's regs. All ground troops have to be 'adequately outfitted for the field'. Some of us were lucky and got real ones issued. The squad leader, Perez, over there," he said as he pointed at a man indistinguishable from the next who was leaning against the side of their vehicle, waiting, with his weapon slung across his torso, eyes with heavy sleep lines under them, nodding off. "He spent his whole first paycheck to buy his. I wish I'd thought of that."

Madeline heard the captain call her over.

"Thanks," she said to the young man, wishing she could think of something else more profound.

The man spat on the ground some distance next to him. A brownish wad splattered on the dirt.

"Try not to get us killed," was his answer.

Madeline walked away, confused as to why the man was so outright aggressive toward her.

"Good chat?" Captain asked.

"I don't think he likes me."

Captain blew out a sharp exhale from his nostrils.

"Old animosity; officially, Ordnance is more important than grunts. For *you,* though, your little reputation precedes you and they don't want to die trying to save your life."

"I didn't ask them to."

"*You* didn't. Don't forget that we all took an oath. Say they don't want to do their job, what happens then?"

Madeline knew.

"Dishonorable discharge."

"A year ago, maybe. Now it's prison."

She had nothing to say to the revelation, and instead opened a can of Amp Energy to keep her mind alert. The captain seemed unusually tired. Though, it could have been his normal demeanor. She saw him so infrequently that she could not be sure. Their last full conversation had been a reprimand over her hastiness in recovering a tactical robot and destroying an egg cluster. To be kind, she offered an unopened Amp Energy can to the captain. He refused.

"Those give me kidney stones," he said.

"Just one can't hurt, can it?" she insisted.

A fly landed briefly on the edge of his eyebrow, and he scratched the skin there.

"Imagine trying to piss a rock out of your ass," he said, which made no sense to Madeline. "I'm not touching that stuff."

She put the can into her backpack and went to the back of the UTAV to place it in an open seat. When she returned, the captain was checking the engine. At the risk of being an annoyance, she walked up to him.

"You want me to drive this time?" she asked, ready to begin the day and eager to try her skills at driving the UTAV. Thus far, she had only driven a handful of times when her superiors were either not present or keen to rest in the passenger seat.

"Sergeant will. You can on the way back," he said.

The sky began to clear as the sun peeked up from the horizon. Goodway approached, and soon after so did Rostein and the sergeant.

They went through the usual tasker summary, which rarely changed, and soon they were on route to survey a path that they would take out into the unknown vastness of the land. To an untrained eye, it seemed identical to any other in the landscape, but for the small differences that she saw through the grace of her optic lenses. Some she could mark already as small black dots in a field of brown, others were hidden well, and she would have to tread carefully.

The convoy halted and Madeline and her team jumped out of the UTAV to the road below. Madeline walked to a spot that had been previously cleared and saw no trace of any re-spawned Mites. She squatted and held her face close to the ground to scrape at the dirt with her bare hands. Her eyes searched the area but found nothing except for a hole the size of a fist nestled between two rocks. She stood to wipe her dirty hands on the sides of her pants and looked over to the scattered Oversight, to her own team, and saw as they each scoured the ground for signs of tampering until, one by one, they rose and would shake their heads at her.

"Nothing," Goodway informed.

Madeline nodded and walked to where Perez stood so she could relay the message. He nodded in acknowledgement, and they all returned to their respective vehicles and moved farther along until they returned to a section near the worn farmland. The Oversight once again stood in waiting with their rifles and surveyed every inch of the area while Madeline and her team searched the land with sharpened eyes. Cockroaches called in the distance somewhere in the tops of the rustling branches. Their guttural songs haunted the terrestrial land in a full-hearted caroling. She moved over the rocks and stones like a passing mist until she stopped. It was all but silent until a low boom erupted in the distance. The Oversight shouted out commands. Each one of the team heard the commands. As they had been trained to do a thousand times over, they drew their weapons, found cover, and scanned the area for threats. Quite a distance down from where they hunkered, a small group of soldiers returned fire in echoing succession. Soldiers bellowed orders, codes, and abbreviations of which Madeline could barely pay attention to amid racketing bullets.

Madeline glanced over her cover at the action. Small, uniformed bodies rushed ahead in formation, firing at the gelatinous figures that threatened them. They looked like toy soldiers in the dirt. It took only moments until there was silence once more. Madeline stood up and went back to the road where the Oversight soon re-emerged. The squad leader descended back down the hill and walked straight towards Madeline. He breathed heavily. Drops of sweat rolled down from his forehead that he wiped with a dirty hand, causing a smeared brown patch on his skin. When he got close enough, he stopped just in front of Madeline and stooped over so that he could glare at her like a parent scolding a child.

"They're gone, so can you *hurry* it up here?" he said with a scowl.

I'm trying to do my job, Madeline thought. She stared back at him and parted her lips, ready to challenge him.

She stopped when she noticed his smell: dirt, sweat, and burnt ammunition. He and his team had protected hers.

It's not worth fighting over, she decided. She nodded once at him and returned to her position. The Oversight had since taken up their positions once more as their eyes scanned the landscape. If small arms fire were any indication, she was sure that there would be a Mite somewhere along the side of the road. She shifted her eyes over each skeletal bush and fallen branch. Her sights paused over a small tip of what looked like a gritty plant root sticking up from the dust underfoot. She squatted and gently brushed away the dirt.

Madeline went to work. Then she heard a sound that she knew all too well. For a moment, she feared that her own foot had met the mark, but the vulgar noise was too far off to have been detonated from her own position. Madeline glanced over her shoulder. Fragments of dust drifted down. All that remained was the silence and the soil. She turned back to the exposed tentacles of a Mite and marked it before she rushed over with quick but careful steps along the length of road.

On the ground lay Rostein, though she was almost unrecognizable. Her face was a bloated, bruised, purple, with white streaks across it that looked like lightning scars. A Mite grasped at her neck with spiked tentacles. Madeline muttered a curse. Her heart beat with adrenaline. She tried to remain calm even though her hands shook.

"Rostein!?" she asked.

Rostein responded with a weak whimper.

What can I do? Madeline thought. She was frozen. Rostein wasn't supposed to get hurt. No one was. *I had it under control. It should've been fine.*

Madeline fixated on what just happened and tried searching her mind for a solution. She couldn't think of one. Her mind was blank.

Think! Do something! She told herself as she stared dumbfounded at the scene. *Why can't I think?*

Madeline wasn't sure how long she remained frozen until, at last, she caught hold of a single thought.

Control panic, she remembered the field manual.

Madeline took a deep breath and exhaled to calm her rapid heartbeat. She took up her radio and keyed the channel to call for a medical helicopter. She managed to give the location and then there was static. She cursed again.

I hope they got that, she thought.

They would have to wait until the helicopter arrived to take Rostein back.

"You're alright. I'm here," she said. At that moment, she wished she knew Rostein's first name.

Madeline checked Rostein's breathing. It was haggard but constant. To open the airway farther, Madeline grasped Rostein's lower jaw at either side and gently moved it forward. Rostein's breathing deepened and calmed. The next step required discipline.

Madeline's hand went to the knife on her belt. She slid it from the sheath and flipped the blade out. Pressing one hand gently on Rostein's neck, she held the tip of the blade to the tentacles. She was not a medic. She never learned anything beyond her basic job skills in training. She might make things worse, but she couldn't sit and do nothing while Rostein writhed in agony. She tried to find a wedge between where Rostein's skin ended, and the Mite's began. She slid the knife tip flat, wriggled it between skins, then turned the blade upward. She made a single, strong, upward jerk, to cut the tentacle at the base. The Mite reacted by retracting. It curled its other tentacles inward around its own body. Its skin created sharp protrusions that dropped off onto the ground.

She wanted to move Rostein to the UTAV. Madeline lifted her shoulders gently but at the pained groan coming from Rostein's mouth, she stopped. After minutes that seemed to last hours, a medical helicopter arrived with technicians. As they settled her carefully on the stretcher, Madeline found herself staring at Rostein's gashed leg, unable to tear her gaze from the bloodied mess that it was. They lifted Rostein off the ground and her injured foot moved in a way that was un-human. It looked like a marionette's leg when the performer slacked the line, and the leg was left to dangle on its own.

Madeline clenched her jaw at the sight of it, thankful that her comrade could not see it for herself. They pulled Rostein into the helicopter and quickly rose into the air.

Goodway returned to report. Madeline briefly explained what happened to which Goodway's reply was a slow nod. Madeline turned to the spot where Rostein had been and to where the pieces of the Mites remained. She took a breath and stored the pieces to bring back to the base where they would be assessed later.

Though Rostein had been taken to safety, their own task was not yet complete. She and Goodway had to gather their composure quickly to reassess the roadway for any other signs. The time went by as slowly as their feet moved while searching the ground. She looked to Goodway, afraid for a moment that he would skip in his step and suffer a worse fate than their comrade. But her steps were sharper than before, honed in a way that could only be caused by the sudden realism of the scattered death all around her.

Madeline spotted another one and called it out. She went to the side coffers of the UTAV to remove additional fuses and the instruments of her trade. She stood once more before it, laid the tools on the ground and took a small field notebook and a pen from the large pocket on her left thigh. She flipped the cover over on the spiral rings and began to swiftly jot down formulas. The calculations ran through her mind while she wrote them down on the paper to judge the blast radius. She re-calculated three times to ensure that the number satisfied her, then showed the captain. He nodded, looked over to the Oversight squad leader and called her over.

"That one is going to be big, so we'll need to back the convoy up about five hundred meters. They probably wanted to have us run over this one," Captain Green said.

Madeline instructed Goodway to move the UTAV back as she prepared. The other vehicles in the convoy distanced themselves farther away and dismounted once more. She fed the lengthened wire back down the road. Goodway had the detonator prepared for her to wind the wires around. Madeline pressed the button on her radio to make the call. Moments later, a mound of earth discharged a great column of dirt into the air.

Once she deemed the roadway safe, the Oversight team packed up and returned to base beneath the dimming evening sky.

9

She needed sleep. How long had she been awake? She couldn't remember. The adrenaline had not left her yet. Her muscles were still tense and ached. She hadn't bothered to remove her lenses or her uniform. She smelled of sweat and musk, but she didn't care.

Madeline kept hearing the sizzling whispers as she imagined tentacled spines grasping her arm. She rubbed her skin to ensure it was still human. Restlessness made her stand and walk to the door. Before she could think beyond the whispers, she was in the clinic asking to see Rostein.

"It's past visiting hours," the man at the desk said.

Visiting hours were during the day when she would be out in the field. The man scrutinized her name badge, then her face.

"You with Ordnance?"

"Yeah," she said proudly, hoping that it would give her the privilege of bending the rules.

Instead, he said, "You can't keep those in for so long." He put his forefinger to the lid under his eye and made a single, purposeful, swipe, "They're already getting purple."

Madeline didn't like him telling her what to do, so she left, and wandered. Wanting in that moment to talk to her sister, her mother, her father, anyone, she went to the community center door. She opened it and walked purposefully to the telephones lining the wall. As before, there was a line behind the single phone. Not wanting to wait, she tried the other telephones. Each time she put a receiver to her ear, there was nothing. She heard snickers from those in the line and turned around to leave.

Returning to her room, she turned the television on. She desired distraction, even if it was interrupted by static and delays. After a thorough shower to cleanse the grit and sweat, she removed her contacts to place them in the container. With her naked eyes exposed, she had to squint against the light. Her eyes watered, irritated at the change in scheme. She looked at them in the mirror. The man had been correct. The rims around her eyes were a dull, bruised purple.

Madeline sat on her bed, pulled out a pen and notebook, and began writing a letter. After three pages, her restlessness faded, her eyelids closing involuntarily. She fell asleep on the bed, still covered by a towel with the sporadic television murmuring in the background.

She found herself awakened abruptly by the familiar tone of the telephone sounding off. The call was always the same. She squinted against the neon red numbers that read 12:30, grunted at the hour, and forced herself to rise in bed.

Can't they take a day off?

With the rising temperatures, night hours became more common. It helped to stave off heat exhaustion but came with the added difficulty of trying to spot Mites in the darkness. She blinked several times to correct her blurry vision, replaced the contacts, and quickly dressed in yesterday's uniform and tied her boots. She took up her gear that sat next to the door: the backpack, vest, and belt that all clinked together when she heaved it onto her shoulders.

Madeline felt a slow anxiousness thrumming inside her chest. Her thoughts rested on Rostein and on whether she would make the same mistake. With a deep breath, she donned her heavy helmet, and her backpack, and stepped out into the dark morning. Madeline made sure to stop at the vending machines to fill her backpack with snacks and Amp Energy, though when she tried the latter, the inventory was empty. It would be a rough day without the reliable boost. She stood in line at the armory. The others there were quiet though there were always one or two who were perky and chatted amongst themselves. Madeline was too exhausted to notice what was being said, barely registering the voices as more than background noise. At her turn, she showed her card and received her weapon before sluggishly walking out to meet the rest of her team. As she walked, she periodically flicked her eyes up to the sky to spot the twinkling stars.

Once reaching the convoy, Sergeant James gave Madeline a map and told her to drive. Their destination was near Lake Superior, and they would arrive at night. Nevertheless, Madeline took the driver's seat of the UTAV while Goodway sat in the passenger seat. She was ready to drive when the sergeant told her to wait.

Just then, a figure walked towards them. It was Rostein. Madeline felt the thrumming once more and looked away.

"Out already?" Goodway asked.

"Just a few scratches," she said dismissively. "Gave me Motrin and said I was good to go."

Madeline wanted to talk to her, but Rostein passed by to join them inside. Madeline gave Goodway the map so she could focus on driving and he on navigating.

In the vehicle, a putrid musk settled within; the scent of sweat and dirt and the inability to be clean of it. The dust from the road settled on the windshield to create a blurry scene. She looked out into the dark landscape. The headlights were bright so she hoped that would be enough to prevent her from driving into a wall of tentacles. She had to drive slowly. Hidden beneath them could be hundreds of Mites waiting to be discovered. This task was dull. When she said so, Goodway scoffed.

"Which is worse," he began, "The craziness yesterday or walking around doing nothing? I'd rather be doing nothing."

They spoke together infrequently in these dark hours as Madeline followed his map navigation. The heat had its way of sapping their focus. More than once she had to slap her cheeks to keep awake.

"Do you have any Amp?" she asked Goodway. When she closed her mouth, she realized that she had not brushed her teeth. She would have to chew gum later. Though, how much did it matter? They all stunk.

"No. The machine was out when I got there."

Madeline groaned. She asked Rostein, who did not answer. A glance in the rearview mirror showed Rostein hunched over a mobile device. The screen glowed, casting a blue light on her face.

"I have caffeine shots," Goodway offered.

Goodway rummaged through his own backpack and handed her a tiny plastic cup, barely three inches tall, with a vacuum sealed plastic top. She glanced back quickly to make sure she grabbed the can, which made her swerve. She centered the vehicle once she had the drink in hand. Madeline pushed her thumb nail into the mouth of the lid to open the can, inadvertently spilling a few drops on her thumb. She consumed the entirety in a single gulp. It was surprisingly sweet. Madeline dropped the empty container on the floorboard.

"I haven't seen those around," she said.

"My wife sent them."

Madeline was stunned and had to remind herself to keep the wheel straight. Goodway had never mentioned a family, and he never wore a wedding band.

"Wife?!" came Rostein from the back. "You never said you were married. How long have we been here, and you never talked about a wife?"

"You didn't ask," he replied.

"Then why don't you wear a ring?" Rostein accused.

"It kept getting caught on the gloves."

Rostein scoffed.

Other than the sergeant laughing, there was silence at the flippant remark.

"Do you have a picture of her? I've got to see the kind of woman that would marry *you*."

Goodway pushed himself up so he could reach the wallet in his back pocket. He opened the wallet so Rostein could see. Madeline took turns shifting her focus from the road to Goodway as she tried to glimpse the picture.

"That's not at all what I had in mind. I thought she would be fifty years old, at least. And is she pregnant?"

"Yes," he said, pride clear in his voice, "Little Charles Louis Goodway, the Third."

He returned his wallet to his pocket. Madeline regretted not insisting on sneaking a look at it.

"I almost got married," Rostein said, "Engaged and everything, then I went on deployment and things fell apart. Listen, Mad," She tapped Madeline's shoulder, "Military and marriage don't mix," said Rostein.

Goodway preferred to ignore her comment, and instead looked at the map again and told Madeline to stop in a few hundred meters. She slowed to a stop at a determined spot and engaged the emergency brake.

With the others, she went to work in the usual way that had lost its initial fervor. She walked, searched, and found Mites. As she waited to set up the controlled detonation, she looked up at the starry sky. In that brackish ocean, a tiny white orb burned. Jupiter. It hovered in the lonely space near Cancer. The other stars were pinpricks beside it. How insignificant she seemed, gazing up at the aeonic being. Madeline detonated and the Mite dissipated. She performed the same motions on other Mites until the darkness relinquished to the dawn. Once finished, the ground was spotted with dead Mites, she collected the remains in the biohazard case and returned to the vehicle.

As Madeline and Rostein removed their armor, she noticed that Goodway remained near the lakeside with his head down. She worried that he had found something she may have overlooked. Madeline approached, squinted against the sunrise, and waved away the waking mosquitos. Clouds swept towards them like a shadow over the ground, enshrouding and voiding the landscape of light. It was as if a great godly hand enclosed itself on the world to shut out the brightness of the sun. The sun shone high somewhere above the muggy dust that hung in the air for hours. Lake Superior stood before her. The once large body of water had dwindled over the generations and was little more than a small lake. If she had a boat, she could row from one end to the other with ease. Along the terrain were hills of rocks and shrubs. Each stone was covered in the sandy dust that coated everything.

"Did I miss one?" she asked.

He shook his head, then squatted and used his forefinger to push some of the pebbles.

"I'm looking for a kind of rock," he said.

He picked one up, tossed it aside, then inspected another. His lips curled into a triumphant smile. To Madeline the rock looked like all the others.

"A rock?"

"A Petoskey stone," he clarified. "You can only find them around these lakes."

He slipped it in his pocket and pottered around some more. Rostein had done the same. As Madeline thought about it, it reminded her of being in school. With no other entertainment in the classrooms, she and her friends would often make their own fun to stave off boredom, whether that had been rolling eraser shavings into tiny balls to throw at each other or scribbling on desktops. There was no entertainment but what they made for themselves. At war, it was no different.

"You're ending up like Rostein," Madeline said.

"At least rocks can't bite you," he said.

She laughed.

"You look for rocks, Rostein looks for bugs," she paused. "I look at the stars."

"Gotta find something worthwhile to do in this place," he said.

"Blowing up Mites isn't fun enough for you?"

He shrugged. Watching him assess the stones around the lake reminded her of her father, though they neither looked nor acted anything alike.

"What do they look like?" she asked, mildly interested.

Goodway picked up a stone and tossed it, so it skipped across the water's surface.

"Gray. It's got hexagons and little dark spots."

Madeline glanced around.

"They're all gray," she pointed out.

"That's the challenge," he answered.

Madeline blinked and rubbed her sore eyes.

"Let's get back," she said.

They returned to the UTAV, beyond ready to return to the base. They placed the cordoned material for disposal in the vehicle. They removed their gear but made sure to keep their armored vests secure. Madeline opened the vehicle door. A waft of hot air met her and reached behind the seat to find her backpack. Under some empty food packets, she found an old can of Amp Energy she forgot was there. She smiled at the discovery. She hefted herself into the driver's seat. It was a near impossible task to pull the seat belt around her vest, but she managed it. She started it, took a gulp of the hot liquid, and made a crude sound of disgust at the temperature's sensation on her tongue. Goodway took the passenger seat. When he sat, he exhaled, and wiped the sweat from his forehead and neck.

"Here." She gave him the can.

He took it, drank without reaction, and gave it back.

"It's too hot to be out here," he said.

Sergeant James was last to enter and took a seat behind them.

"Let's go," she said, then checked the watch on her wrist, "I want to try to catch the game."

"Football or Baseball?" Madeline asked, thinking of her school's sports teams.

"Hockey," she answered.

"*Tch.* You'll barely see anything with the reception we got," Goodway said.

"Better than nothing," Sergeant said.

Madeline started driving. She turned on the air conditioning fan, hoping it would alleviate the heat. All it did was blow hot air in her face.

"Yeah, that's broken," Sergeant said.

She turned it off and kept driving. Besides the sound of the engine, the inside of the vehicle was quiet. Sergeant slept in the back and Goodway scrolled through his handheld mobile device. Concentrating on the road made Madeline's eyelids begin to droop. She drank from her can then blinked several times, trying to force her eyes to stay open.

There was a loud pop and a bright red flash. A plume of dirt and sand rose in the air in front of them, tossing large rocks into the windshield and throwing the vehicle violently forward onto its topside.

10

Madeline's ears rang. Her head whipped backwards. She lurched forward and her hands and forearms smashed against the windshield. Her head throbbed uncontrollably, blurring her vision. She blinked several times to correct her vision. When her vision cleared, she looked around. Everything was skewed at an awkward angle. The windshield was damaged beyond repair. Shattered glass intermingled with dirt across the dashboard.

Think, she willed. Madeline was quiet as she absorbed the situation. In the next moment, she screamed in frustration. She hit the driving wheel with an open palm, leaving it dirtied and spotted with blood. She pressed the call button on her radio, reporting the occurrence to anyone listening. The voice that emerged on the other end was broken and ragged as the transmission cut off in places. She steadied a hand on the roof and unbuckled. With a gentle thump, she rolled onto her back and then into a sitting position. She checked her watch for the time. Madeline looked over to Goodway and Rostein. Goodway was already out of his seat and sitting against the inside of the door. Rostein was still buckled in and upside down.

"Is everyone okay?!"

Goodway grunted, "Ah," he breathed "I think so. Goddamn."

He touched the superficial cuts to his face and then to his nostrils where his slightly swollen and bent nose dribbled blood down his lips and chin. He wiped his nose with his sleeve which had the effect of smearing some blood across his upper lip.

Madeline peered back at the sergeant, who was still intact, and restrained in her seat.

"I don't like the idea of being out here for too long." Sergeant said in such a calm tone that Madeline thought she imagined it.

Sergeant unbuckled, careful to steady herself as she did so, then said, "How long until relief comes? Did you catch it?"

"Not really," Madeline said.

She picked up the radio to call again. All she heard was static.

Sergeant cursed.

"We'll have to stay here until they show up. Good work getting the first call through," she said to Madeline. "I'll check the rig."

Madeline unbuckled and then looked down at her hands. Both were cut deep with gashes. Slivers of glass from the broken windshield stuck out from her knuckles. She could not feel any pain. She laughed and nodded to Goodway.

"You're not much of a picture."

Goodway turned upside down to look at his reflection in the upturned rearview mirror.

"Well, Mom always said I should get a nose-job," he quipped. He turned from the mirror and began rustling in the back of the vehicle.

Rostein chuckled and then ceased.

"Ow," she said and sucked in her breath. "I think my ribs are busted."

Madeline looked at her. Besides a cut on her forehead, she was intact. Rostein moved her hand to the seat belt buckle.

"Don't move," Madeline advised, remembering her field manual's segment on injuries. "Let me help."

Madeline shifted closer and positioned her hands under Rostein's armpits. She groaned when the pressure of Rostein's weight rested on her injuries. Once she pressed the button that released her seat belt, Madeline steadied Rostein onto the roof.

"Here's the kit," Goodway said, and placed the first aid kit where they could all reach it.

When he opened it, he took gauze and wiped his nose enough to sop up a decent amount of blood. It was not enough to clean it thoroughly and left red streaks.

"Hand me the tweezers," Madeline said.

She tried to pull out the shards by herself, though her hands trembled and kept missing the finer pieces.

Rostein watched her try and fail before she took the tweezers and told Madeline to "Hold still," as she removed shards of glass. She twitched each time the tweezers nipped her skin. Her hands began to sweat so she would periodically wipe them on her pants.

The inside of the vehicle became increasingly suffocating. She could not sit any more. Not in the crashed vehicle. Considering the situation, she did not want to make an irrational mistake like she had done before. There was a standard protocol: in the event of a vehicle accident or collision, stay in the vehicle unless there was the threat of explosion or an enemy attack. But Madeline couldn't sit still.

Well, if Sergeant James can get out, why not me?

"I'm getting out of this thing," Madeline announced.

She tried to open the door but found that it would not move. She grunted her weight into it until it finally unlatched and swung open. Madeline struggled to climb out of the UTAV while the heaviness of her vest constrained her breathing. Madeline surveyed the outside quickly before jumping out. All that remained in the area was the endless dirt road Madeline walked to join her. As soon as she turned in front of the vehicle, she saw that the entire left half of it was torn apart. Twisted remains hung off the front.

Rostein remained inside the vehicle. Madeline stretched her fingers and winced from some tiny shards still lodged in unseen places. She looked back at Rostein who had pulled her notebook and pen from her calf pocket to note the blast damage. Her wrist flicked as she quickly jotted down a post-blast analysis.

Despite the excitement, her stomach growled. She looked past Rostein to where her backpack would have been behind her seat, but which was crushed under the shifted contents inside the vehicle. Madeline rubbed her eyes and groaned, disgruntled that she would have nothing to eat. Then, she remembered the ready meal that Sergeant James had given her the first time she went out in the field and asked Rostein to find it under the seat.

"As long as I get the candy," Rostein said.

Before giving the brown package over, Rostein rummaged through it and took the candy packet for herself. Madeline stood outside. She opened a meal packet labeled, "Cheese Tortellini" and began eating it with the pre-packaged plastic spoon that had a split down the center. The taste was bland but not terrible.

As she ate, she looked over to where the convoy vehicles had already ceased. A single Marine team leader jogged over to Sergeant James.

"You call it?" the Marine asked.

"We got through about fifteen minutes ago. This is too busted for combat repairs," Rostein said from inside. "They'll have to tow it back."

"Alright. We'll standby here until they get back."

The Marine nodded once before jogging back to the vehicle.

Madeline finished her food then tossed the rest of the packets back inside the vehicle. She moved back to the side of the damaged UTAV where Rostein and Goodway stood guard with their weapons at the ready. Rostein looked at her team leader with her eyebrows furrowed.

There was nothing to do but wait.

Madeline removed a pack of disposable vapor cigarettes from her breast pocket and put one to her lips.

Goodway chuckled, "Give one here."

Madeline inhaled and blew out the smoke. She handed the box to him and when he took one of the cigarettes, he gave it back. Madeline rubbed her forehead, trying to soothe the mild headache that emerged. Her ears rang with a low hum. Goodway stood propped up next to the shade that the vehicle cast down on the ground, his left leg propped out in front of him, and his body weight leaned to his right side. He held out his weapon in front of his chest. From her radio she heard a call tone. Madeline jumped at the sound and pressed the button.

"Relief should be there in about two hours. Over."

"Copy."

Madeline glanced at her watch. She informed the sergeant, whose response was a disgruntled mumble. Madeline shut the engine cover and climbed back into the back of the vehicle.

"It'll be a few hours until we can head out again."

Goodway took one last inhale and returned the cigarette to Madeline. She turned to grab it and then something caught her attention. She looked past Goodway's shoulder and saw them.

At first there was a flicker of movement, then she recognized the horrible, lumbering charge of mindless bodies. Each one had a quivering luminescence in rainbow hues that dulled to black and violet as they came closer. They were almost human from a distance. She could convince herself of that when seeing their forms. Yet as they came closer, their alienation was apparent. Their skin did not fit their bodies. On some it was too flabby. It hung off them, pulling their faces down to reveal the red skin underneath. Others had skin so tight that it stretched across their muscles to show their veins and bones. Still more were contorted into odd positions. It seemed impossible that they should walk, or even move at all. One in particular seemed like a skeleton had been forced into the body of a squid. There were tendrils erupting from all parts. The top of the head was abnormally large, as if the brain had swollen and was about to burst. There were legs and arms bent and contorted backwards so that when it moved it did so on splayed knees and elbows. Some still had fragments of clothing fused to their bodies. On all of them were blisters and emotionless faces.

Madeline looked higher, above the horizon, to the gargantuan creature hovering in the dusky sky. If she did not have her optic lenses, she would not have seen it. To her, it shone bright blue in the center, and the outline a fluorescent green. It nearly blended in, like a cloud of smog. It looked not unlike a cuttlefish, though with longer tendrils and a more menacing stature.

There was only one reason a Damocles Spear was traveling, and that was to assimilate territory.

Madeline cursed, which drew Goodway's attention. She took out her radio.

"Report: A Damocles Spear and about twenty Mites coming up on us. We need extra relief. Copy," she said as calmly as she could, though her heartbeat raced.

"Copy that. We'll call another Oversight crew to your location. Standby."

"Copy. Out," she acknowledged.

They were a steady rolling wave. Any more relief would take some time to mobilize. Ordnance were support, not impact troops. They were never meant to face combat. Their weapons were meant for light combat, for picking off one or two of them, not fighting back a horde.

I have to do something, Madeline thought.

She went to the overturned vehicle where Goodway was already searching for weapons. They had a handful of magazines and two more combat rifles. All three took cover behind the UTAV. When she saw them, Madeline fired in bursts. Bulbous nodules burst like rotten peaches, spilling thick ooze in all directions. Pieces of bodies spewed above and around them, sticking to spots on their uniform. Goodway shouted. Madeline snapped her head over to see one of the dismembered tentacles fused to three of his fingers. He dropped his weapon. For no more than a few seconds, Goodway remained motionless. Madeline was ready to rush over to him with her knife. Before she could, he clasped his free hand over the tentacle and ripped it off, taking some layers of skin with it.

"Are you alright?" Madeline asked.

Goodway looked at her and nodded, though his eyes were wider than before, and his hand was bleeding. He picked up his weapon. Madeline turned back to the creatures.

More terrifying than the vision of them approaching was the great silence with which they did so. The only sound in the expanse was from continuous firing while they advanced. Madeline's bolt locked back, signaling that her magazine was empty. She rushed to the back of the vehicle to search for more ammunition. There was none.

"You have a magazine?" Madeline asked Goodway hastily.

"Yeah," Goodway hollered, seeing that there were more creatures lumbering towards them. He handed her a full magazine from his belt. She loaded and fired more rounds.

"This is insane," Rostein said.

"Yeah?" Madeline asked. "Well, what else can we do?"

"You ever think about leaving?" Rostein asked.

Madeline pointed at their mangled vehicle. "How d'you think we can do that?'

"Run?"

Goodway scoffed. "All the way to base?"

"Then we could hide."

"We're S.O.L no matter what," Goodway said. "But if we retreat, we might be able to meet up with relief."

"I'm not leaving," Madeline said and fired into the expanse. "If you wanna go, then go."

Goodway stared at her quizzically. "You don't need to stay."

"Yes, I do," Madeline said as she gave a cocky smirk. "Besides, they don't call me 'Mad' for nothing."

Goodway patted her on the shoulder once. Rostein gave her an extra magazine from her belt and said, "I'll see you soon."

Madeline watched for a few spared moments as they sprinted away from her.

Be safe, she thought.

Madeline turned back to the enemy and fired where she could. But they were too fast and came upon her too suddenly. She kept firing and once her rifle was empty, she used the weapon to bludgeon the beasts. When she hit, the impact did nothing but create a slight ripple. She had not been so close to one of the creatures before. There was a brain inside the skull; a being that was once human behind the bulbous skin. She wanted to believe that there was something of humanity to be saved in it— some spark not yet extinguished.

She pulled back from their touch and was met with resistance. Instinct told her to retreat but she did not want to move away. She could not. Curious to discover what they may be and too apathetic to care if they would kill her remaining humanity. Her skin changed color. It pulsated like a squid while emitting bioluminescent patterns. The colors mesmerized Madeline. As she watched, she struggled to decipher the cryptic signals.

She could only move so far until the tentacles encompassed the side of her face, forcing her to look into its fractal eyes. For a moment, they seemed sympathetic, and on the verge of tears. The luminescence moved in rhythmic patterns. Blue and pink shades waved in alternating angles. It was telling her something, but she could understand only fragments, like listening to someone speaking in broken syntax and mixed grammar. Concentrating, she gleaned the most basic meaning.

Oneself pain is not, it said in a voice like a whisper in her ear.

Snippets of events passed over her, overlaying one by one into a visual narrative. It came all at once, overwhelming her. Each image, each movement was indecipherable from the next with no semblance of linearity.

She was in clear water. White sunlight spread overhead. She moved by stretching muscular tentacles to traverse the shallow waters. There were others with her, heading upward, grasping shoals with suckers. She met their overly large horizontal eyes with rectangular pupils. Their initially smooth blue skin contracted into bumps, then changed to project a multitude of orange rings across its bruised violet body. It was a warning. She understood and rotated to look behind her.

Her body became heavy with the touch of the creature. Gravity pulled her far into the subterranean. A smell of brine and blood. A figure she guessed as female. A round stomach, full fleshed skin, placid face. That same cephalopod skin, shimmering.

Changing woman, came a thought.

Asdzaa Nádleehé, Madeline remembered from the stories her mother told her. She was the languid and beautiful woman who tore pieces from her own skin to create men and women.

Madeline's ears filled with water. The dirt that once surrounded her was washed away by a wave that enshrouded her in a warm embrace. The sky darkened and when she raised her head it was as if she gazed up at the sun from far below the surface of the sea. The depths were a dark nebula; billowing black clouds roiled into the violet darkness where sunbeam halos burn the outer edges. White debris that were as snowflakes in the water disintegrated the farther they fell.

A wraithlike rhythm emerged with a soft trilling that flooded her senses like the movement of a fish breathing underwater and of rolling appendages gliding over rough undersea stones. Madeline moved towards them, these large creatures that brought a mysterious intelligence. Their colors pulsated. Their skin morphed into odd shapes that made whatever they were trying to convey difficult to understand. With outstretched tentacles, they exchanged blood and venom in symbiosis.

She learned to walk on their eight legs. She caught a crab and pulverized it in her beak. There were more like her. A fusion of Helgrammaw walked on strange lands. In that unmanned space, they were free to evolve.

They met a human child. Instinct told them to embrace the unknown welcomingly, as their ancestors had done. This was the best way to cooperate, to create. They embraced the child and it made noises they had never heard and emitted foreign smells from its unchanging skin.

From one birthed hundreds. Eggs spawned into random genuses of Mites. She watched as Engineers like her destroyed them. They angered at the genocide of their offspring. The creatures would do whatever they could to defend themselves from the violent humans.

We can give them peace, came a thought sensation. *Through symbiosis, humans will not fear us; they will become us, become better. Is humanity worth saving?*

She pondered this. Earthen life was in a constant state of fluctuation. In comparison to other creatures who came before, humans had been a speck on the page of planetary history. What had they accomplished in that time? What was their legacy?

Intelligence, civilization, kindness, relationships, war, hatred, murder. Pandora's riddle. Humans were endangered. Humans as she was. She wanted to remain, but they stole that from her. Tried to turn her into one of them. She had not wanted it. Humanity was her. Without it, even though her heart still beat, she was dead. Perhaps she did not need to be. There were other memories, those that did not belong to her, but were being shared through their skin. Humans had once been different until millennia of evolution, inter-species reproduction changed them. Did it matter what would come after them?

She shook the intrusive thoughts away.

They were trying to manipulate her to think as they did. She remembered the Ashfall and the constant advance of the Helgrammaw. They razed cities and transformed all the marks of human civilization into their subterranean world.

A burning cold shook the breath from Madeline's lungs. She fought it but at each touch came the painful shock. A white bolt that seared through her, expunging any thought beyond pain. There was a scream. An inhuman scream. Whether it came from her or another, she could not tell, only that it pierced her eardrums. Then all at once, it ceased, and she was free.

Until she opened her eyes, she had not realized that they had been closed. The creature remained unmoving before her. It stared blankly into the air ahead then suddenly animated. It turned to join the remaining compatriots who were moving together in a populous flank. Madeline felt as if she had a steadily rising fever. With it came a dizziness that forced her to collapse onto the ground.

Her vision blurred. She tried to blink it into focus. Everywhere, her skin prickled. The epicenter of the burn focused on her right eye. She shouted. No answer. She dragged herself to the side mirror on the overturned vehicle to gauge her curiosity. The iris bubbled. Her bio-optics sizzled as they melted into her pupil. It felt as if spider legs were tickling the inside of her iris. A greater fear grew when she looked at the rest of her face. Her skin began to change rapidly. The normal flesh became pale and undulating. When she pulled back her sleeve, she watched as the hives spread up her arm. Trying to capture a coherent thought was difficult.

Her veins filled with thickening blood as her skin bubbled and rolled. She removed her glove to find her fingers as purple as the juice from a burst blackberry. She leaned closer to the mirror to see her face with her good eye. She blinked several times to clear her vision. The flesh liquefied. Her fingernails grew out from the nail beds then fell off, one by one.

Panic shot through her. A trilling hiss blared in her ears. She had to stop it. She could not die, not when there were so many left to kill. She could not become one of them.

Desperation drove her to the knife at her belt. She inhaled deeply, as if ready to plunge into a bottomless sea. She pressed the knife tip to her lower eyelid. It was so close that it tickled her eyelashes. Her muscles twitched as if protesting her intent. She pressed the blade to her eye. Madeline flinched at the sharpness as it pierced the soft cornea. She watched through the mirror, even as her mutating hand shook. She used her other hand to steady the knife when the shaking became too vigorous. The alien hand refused to cooperate. Her synapses misfired. The orders from her mind dislodged before the extremities received them, causing her fingers to quiver. She willed her hand to obey. She used her free hand to stop it. In the struggle, she pierced her cornea. She gasped, expecting excruciating pain. Instead, there was a loud internal burst. The vision in that eye flashed white and then black. Watery ooze dribbled down her cheek. The odd mucus that wept from her bubbling skin made the handle slippery. She dropped the knife.

Madeline tried looking for it. She squinted to focus. The vision in her remaining eye began to fog from bodily distress. Her hand that continued to respond to her mental commands felt the ground for the knife while her alien arm moved on its own. Skin rippled. Her fingers swelled. It was like thousands of caterpillars were crawling beneath her skin. She had to rid herself of the parasite.

Madeline found the knife. She grabbed it by the blade first and then took it by the handle. She poked at the sleeve of her uniform and cut to reveal the extent of the growing transformation. What she saw made her pick at the skin from her arm with the edge of the knife. Even as she cut away her bubbling human flesh, she felt nothing.

Why can't I feel it? she thought. She chuckled at the ridiculous thought of missing the feeling of pain.

Underneath the dermal layers, she looked like them. Her flesh transformed into grotesque pink skin with soft nodules that pulsated. There was a pungent smell of sea foam that came from the putrefaction.

I can't be like them, she thought.

She would have to amputate to stop the spread. With a raise of her arm to gain strength she aimed the knife point just above the joint. She inhaled deeply in anticipation of pain and jabbed. But there was nothing. Any pain that might have jolted her into submission was gone.

Her vision rapidly sharpened. There were spectrums that she had never seen before. Ultraviolet hues showed her an array of colors previously hidden to her human eyes. It startled her into hesitation. Her attention wavered. She looked towards the sky.

There was a beauty she had never seen before. It was as if she were under the surface of the shallows at sunset. And in the sunset hues were pearl drops glimmering in the fading light. A pearlescent creature floated in the air. Its lithe body shimmered as it swayed with an invisible current. Its tendrils pulsated in iridescent rainbow hues. Madeline had never seen such resplendent skies. It subdued her into a state of tranquility that she never wanted to escape.

11

adeline opened her eye to naked vision. She lifted her fingers to touch her face and felt a bandage shielding the empty eye socket.

Where am I?

She knew the place but struggled to find the correct word. Her brain jumbled from disorientation. She tried to conceptualize her most recent memory. A vehicle, a crash, confusion, and a spectrum of color. That was all.

Hospital, she remembered.

She found an intravenous needle in her arm. The stump was bandaged, stained with watery pink ooze. She wanted to see it and reached to pull the coverings but decided against it at first. She knew it was gone. There was no need to look at it, not yet. She felt an odd ambivalence over the lost limb.

Not lost, she thought, *taken.*

How could a person "lose" a part of their body? It wasn't as if it were snatched by an invisible malevolence. The creatures took it. Yet, it was always a possibility. How many had she already seen maimed before they came for her? There was pride in being among those who suffered for humanity to survive. Nevertheless, a cool despair infiltrated her mind. She had almost turned into one of their ilk. She could hear them, whispering, like the soft undercurrents in a peaceful sea.

Madeline looked around to occupy her mind. She was in her own, small, medical room. There was a clamp on her middle finger that registered her heartbeat. She wondered what day it was. How long had she been asleep? What happened before she was brought here? Were Rostein and Goodway alive? She touched the necklace that still hung in place and stroking the smooth façade.

The door opened. A doctor walked in.

This isn't the same one, she thought.

She could vaguely recall a woman being the first.

Where had that one gone? Busy, probably. I bet they passed her off somewhere down the combat line.

"How do you feel?" This doctor asked. He held a slim digital tablet in one hand and a thin plastic pen in the other.

He was too cheerful for her liking.

"How do I *feel*? Like shit. How d'you think I feel?"

The doctor smiled and said, "I'll just check your vitals."

He went through the clinical procedure. He checked her eye, blood pressure, heart rate, and temperature.

In the hospital bed, alone, and being tended to, she suddenly ached for answers.

"Do you know about my troops?" she asked.

"We have a lot of patients here. Unfortunately, I can't give out information on any other patients, unless you're family."

Family, she thought. *I need them.*

"I want to call my family," she said abruptly. She had been too drowsy with medication to ask before.

"Of course," he said, "there's a phone right here that you can use."

"And I want to see those," she said, pointing at the medical files.

Rather agreeably with a nonchalant smirk, he turned over the tablet to show the full body scans, the brain scans, the nervous system.

It would not likely make any sense to her, but it was her body and her brain. She had a right to see, even if the knowledge was out of her reach. Looking at the scans, she saw nothing out of the ordinary except for the obviously missing limb. There were no signs of an inhuman presence. No malformed organs, no cell damage, no breaks in the bodily systems that were hallmarks of mutation in humans. The brain too was ordinary insofar as she could tell.

So why can I hear them?

"It's all fine," he said when the silence became obvious. "Cutting off the infection seemed to stem the spread. But, in addition to that, x-rays also showed a kidney stone, and your cornea has some scratches and damage, probably from wearing those lenses for too long, so you'll get some eye drops for that."

She took the news without response. She passed back the file, which he took and replaced in the holder.

"After some therapy, you'll be healed up, and sent home."

She did not expect that.

"Medical dismissal?" Madeline asked.

"That's the new policy for any close contact," he said. He brightened his expression by lifting his eyebrows. "You can relax now. The fighting is over."

The fighting isn't over. Just mine, she thought at first. She scoffed.

Don't be so self-pitying.

She felt suddenly aware of her unwashed body. She felt sticky, as if the inside of the hospital had left some invisible film on her skin.

"You can leave now," she said. "I want to clean up."

The doctor nodded, then pointed at a remote on her beside with a single red button. "Push that if you need anything. Do you want help getting up?"

"No," she said quickly. "I can do it myself."

The doctor nodded once. She watched him leave, shut the door, then walk past the thin slat of a window that looked into the hallway.

Madeline pushed herself upright with her one hand and scooted to the end of the bed until her feet just reached the floor. She hopped down and steadied her body as much as she was able. Without her second eye, she had to adjust her balance.

She looked at the plain white bathroom and how normal it seemed. There were tile squares from floor to ceiling, a large bathtub with steel handles and a tiny wedge seat on the inside, a toilet, a sink, and a mirror. As she stared, she let out a small exhale and stretched to turn on the water. She did not wait for it to fill. The steam from the bath fogged the room, making the air suffocating. Madeline undressed carefully. She plunged her feet in and submerged the rest of her body beneath the scalding water.

She clenched her fists to contain the pain that the temperature inflicted on her flesh. She let it burn so that she felt nothing but the scorching heat. She breathed deeply. The humid air enveloped her lungs. Her body convulsed in contact with the scalding water. It calmed her agitation by being able to focus only on one thing. She remained submerged in the water until her body adapted to the cooling temperature. When she sat up in the bath, she saw how her skin reddened from its exposure to the unnatural heat. When she touched her finger to her thigh it left a white mark. She turned off the faucet and tilted her head against the tile to stare at the ceiling. Madeline unfocused her eye so all that she saw was a blur.

There were two of her. One was human, still present on the outside in her skin. She could walk into a store, and no one would find it odd. But there were smaller transgressions that she noticed inside herself. Her heart beat oddly out of sync. Either the doctors had not noticed or had not cared. She had enough of the bath. With some maneuvering, she got out and re-dressed.

When she exited the bathroom, she found Captain Green, the sergeant, Rostein, and even Goodway, still showing signs of healing himself, waiting in the room for her. Seeing them made her nearly lose her balance. Rostein met her to steady her displaced side and help her to her bed. She shirked from Rostein's touch at first, still stained with guilt over failing her, but after a few wobbly steps she submitted to the help.

"It's good to see you," Madeline said.

"You, too. They wouldn't let us visit until now."

"We also didn't want to bother you with this until now," Captain said, "since it took a few weeks to put together."

He handed her a palm-sized black case. Then, the sergeant did the same by handing her a second case.

She opened the first. Inside was a golden star with a small silver star in the center, attached to a red, white, and blue ribbon. He then gave her a tan folder. When she opened it, there was a certificate. She touched the gold filigree laurels around the edges, a golden notary at the bottom, a golden star atop, which all certified that she had been awarded the Silver Star for Gallantry in Action.

She had to touch the medal to ensure it was real. She had been reckless. She had lost a limb. She had done things that seemed smart at the time only to find out that they were mistakes. Her part in the fight had felt simultaneously both excruciatingly long and ferociously short. It did not seem to her that she had yet done enough to earn a commendation. She then looked up to her comrades.

"You sure you're giving it to the right person?" she asked.

Goodway laughed.

"Well, maybe not," he said, "but it's too late to give it to someone else." He leaned his head and lowered his voice. "It also comes with a twenty percent pay increase in your veteran's account. I got one, too."

"Yeah," Rostein added, nodding toward Goodway, "Goodway got himself a Purple Heart. Me, too."

Goodway raised his hand to show where his fingers were bandaged together.

"Looks like you got one," Goodway said, tapping the second case.

When she opened it there was the gold lined Purple Heart with the golden profile of George Washington. Behind the first certificate was a second one, ensuring her receipt of honors.

She thought of the woman she met on the transport to the field--*What was her name?*--who warned her about being a hero.

"I don't want it," she said.

Madeline shut the case. She jumbled the honors together and tossed them to the base of the bed along with her wrinkled sheets.

"Maybe not," Captain said, "So, do what you want with it: keep it, throw it away, hide it in a drawer. Either way, you earned it, despite being--" He turned to Sergeant James. "--how did you describe her to me once?"

"Rambunctious," she answered.

Madeline did not reply. She did not want to look at them. All she wanted at that moment was to roll into herself like a pill bug and disappear under a stone. Her expression must have betrayed her mood, since the captain then said, "We'll give you some time."

Before he left the room together with Sergeant James, Madeline remembered what the doctor told her about having kidney stones.

"You were right about the Amp Energy," she said, with a smile, "I guess I'll find out how it feels to piss out a stone."

The captain laughed, nodded once, and walked out the door. Rostein and Goodway remained while Madeline sat, not knowing what to say.

"I, uh," Rostein started, checking at the window behind her to ensure that they were alone. "I have something for you, too." She took a small object from her pocket and set it on the bed just by her knee. It was a black plastic canister, the size and width of a silver dollar. She opened it. Around the inner edge was what looked like a translucent worm. It was ugly, repugnant, and satisfying. When she picked it up, she turned it, and the worm rolled towards the center. Madeline recognized what it was.

"It's from the one that took your arm. I thought it'd make a good souvenir," Rostein said with a grin.

"How'd you get that?" Goodway asked suspiciously.

"I was on the disposal team, so I cut a slice while no one was looking." She shrugged her right shoulder.

Goodway shook his head and laughed. Madeline felt a wrestling of worry and reverence for her comrade. Keeping a section of biohazardous ordnance was punishable by court martial at best.

Madeline shook the contents, then tucked the canister under her pillow.

Rostein knitted her eyebrows together. "You don't like it?"

"I don't know," she said. "You," she looked up at Rostein, "you're alright?"

"You mean my little scrape?" she asked, "Well, it hurt like all hell, but it looked worse than it was. They fixed me up good."

Rostein lifted her foot onto the end of the bed and pulled up her pant leg. Among the angry red etchings of skin grafts were discolored purple splotches the color of bruised eggplant. Madeline looked away. She felt like she might cry to look at her. It must have been the medication that made her so emotionally sensitive.

"I don't know whether to thank you or twist your arm," she said, "you shanked that thing off me, and since it was--what did command call it?--a 'superfluous wound', there was no reason to keep me out of work for more than three days."

"It was my fault," Madeline blurted suddenly. She felt like a child confessing to breaking a cookie jar after trying to steal a sweet. "I--I didn't clear the road."

She exhaled slowly. "No. You didn't."

Rostein stood up and stretched out her fingers.

"Their fault for putting a kid in the field in the first place," Rostein said. She tapped two fingers twice at her neck where there were still streaked scars, and then pointed at Madeline. "Eye for an eye. They got you, too." Rostein straightened her uniform blouse. "I'd better go get some sleep. I'm out on clearance in the morning."

"Rostein," Madeline said. Rostein paused. "What's your name?"

"Shoshanna," she answered.

Rostein smirked and left without dalliance. With only her and Goodway remaining in the room, she was calmer. Madeline took the trinket from under her pillow. She shook it once more to watch the mass jiggle.

"You hear it, don't you?" She asked him, keeping her gaze on the remains. "The sounds."

He tilted his head to the side.

"A little."

Where her arm used to be was a stump wrapped in thin white bandages. The surrounding skin was naked and showed raw pink skin and red streaks reaching up her shoulder. She recalled the beauty of the sky after their touch.

"Do you remember what you saw, after they touched you?"

He shook his head and crimped his lips. "Not much. Just that it was different. And *they* didn't seem the same."

"It was . . . pretty," she said.

"Yeah," he agreed, "yeah. Except, maybe that's what they want us to think. Change our minds; trick us into thinking that *they're* the good ones." He turned his eyes downward. "I won't believe anything that tries to screw up my brain."

He made a good point. The creatures changed humans and animals to suit their needs. It was logical to assume that they would change their minds as well, to make them sympathetic. However manipulative they might be, they tried to speak with her. Would an insidious enemy do that? They knew so little of the Helgrammaw. Was her doubt the cause of her own conclusions or from their influence? Madeline did not want to think too much about it. If she could not trust her mind, she would have to trust her instincts. Those instincts told her to go to the creatures. To see them for herself. That place was at ground zero. Ashfall.

"I'm going in there."

Goodway glared in disbelief, as if her face were insincere. He did not speak for what seemed to her like several minutes.

When he finally did, he asked, "You still on those pain meds?"

His seriousness of the question made her laugh in earnest. "No. No. I'm not high."

"You got to be, thinking that. I know I call you 'Mad' but you aren't supposed to take it literally."

The smile caused by her laughter began to fade.

"You're serious?" He concluded, then made a disapproving noise caused by exhaling sharply between his teeth. It reminded her of how a camel pulls back its lips before it is about to spit.

She shrugged. "What have I got to lose?"

"You said you had family."

She nodded. Her family would want her home. She wanted to see them, too. Being so busy at her job, she had no time to think of anything else. She thought of the baby. What did baby Eli look like now? He had been so small when they found him alone, crying, strapped in his seat in an abandoned car. Fiona took him, claimed him as her own. How was Fiona? Were her parents healthy? She should try to call them. If she did, what would she say?

"I do. But if I was worried about that, I'd never have joined in the first place."

Her throat became dry, and she swallowed to moisten it. "Besides, since this--" she gestured to his injury and her own, "--I can't stop thinking about them. It's like a--" she glanced away, struggling to find words to describe the sensation. She pointed to her forehead and wagged her fingers as if to play with a wayward string dangling there. "--vibration in there. It's a sound inside my head, just sitting there without going away."

He squinted at her apprehensively.

"Have you told anyone?"

She shook her head.

"I didn't think there was anything to tell. I thought it was just my imagination, but then it never went away," She smiled. "Or maybe it isn't real at all."

She held her palm open in surrender. "What else am I going to do?"

"There's plenty else. Look at me: I'm in the same way as you. They won't take me back after I'm done here. But," he looked at her, and tapped his nose twice. "Early retirement from being wounded in battle, complete with veteran's benefits, and stable pay. I can carve out a nice little life with that."

"What about *them*?"

He shrugged.

"What about them? We did our best; that's all any of us can do. We fought them, and we lost. Maybe our time is up." He looked down. "We've had this place for hundreds of thousands of years. Seems like it should be someone else's turn." He bit the inside of his cheek. "So, for the rest of it I'll spend pissing away my money."

He has a point, Madeline thought. They paid their dues, twice over; they had earned absolution from responsibility. She could not judge him for wanting to indulge. But she could not absolve herself.

"Shouldn't we keep fighting?" she asked, more to herself than to Goodway.

He frowned and shook his head.

"I'm done fighting. There are enough to take my place."

She thought of all the dying, all the changing, and knew it was not true.

"There aren't," she said. "Not enough to make a difference."

He eyed her.

"Stay home. Safe."

"There's nowhere safe."

"That's not what I meant. There's more to do here than *there*. You have family, didn't you say? Go back to them and live the rest of your life doing whatever you want. All of us die at some point. Enjoy what you have left while you can."

"Yeah, you're probably right, or else they wouldn't start taking in troops as young as you."

"Don't we have to do what's right?" she asked. She had a responsibility. She did not want to believe that it was a foregone conclusion.

"I know what's right for me, and that's to get as far from them as I can. I paid my dues. Maybe this is it, for us. And if it is, I'm spending it the way I want. I got a decent discharge reward to use. You should take yours and do something with it--something you enjoy before this entire place is kaput."

Madeline stood abruptly, nearly losing her footing from the rush of blood to her head. She jutted out her hand to grab onto the edge of the headboard. She released a long exhale. There was a great cause. Did it matter?

It has to, she thought. *Or else what was the point of it all?*

She thought of the bodies, some dead, others mutilated, the refugees, the ones like her, holding out for food, listening to hungry babies cry and being powerless to stop the death machine. Did it matter how many she destroyed? There would always be more. She had seen how they replenished, how they grew. Destroying clutches of eggs, detonating Mites, killing and re-killing Mites, was fruitless. There was no technology they had to combat the Helgrammaw, the Damocles Spears.

They could fight, and they did, and all that was left was survival. All that remained of them lived sequestered.

"Have you ever eaten truffles?" he asked.

Madeline shook her head.

"They barely exist anymore. You know how much an ounce of one costs?"

"No."

"Four hundred fifteen dollars."

Four hundred and fifteen dollars. How much food would that have bought baby Eli, or her sister, or her parents?

"What are truffles?" Madeline asked.

"A kind of fungus."

"You want to eat a four hundred and fifteen dollar fungus?" she asked blankly.

Goodway laughed.

"Yeah, I guess so. I'll take my wife out to the most expensive restaurant and buy her truffles, and then retire."

She thought of the Ashfall, containment, moving from refugee homes, joining the military, running from the creatures. Madeline shook her head.

"For what's left of us, we have to fight. You can't hide, not from them. How can you sit here, keeping to yourself, hiding? Fighting back is the only way."

"Is it? What has fighting done but put more humans in graves? They take half, and half more die on the lines. What's left?" His shoulders tightened.

"Then we're like cockroaches."

He tilted his head.

"And cockroaches have existed for millennia."

Madeline narrowed her eyelids. "We should be better than insects. We have to do more than survive." Madeline let out a slow exhale, blinked in one long respite, and relaxed her shoulders. "I can't," she said. "I can't shake a feeling." She looked out as an idea took root. "Has anyone been in the exclusion?"

"I'm sure BioTech has. Most people don't go in there anymore."

Expeditions into their terrain resulted in disappearances, with little useful information gathered. Since electronics were useless in their vicinity, there was no way to closely document their behavior outside of using analog cameras.

Desperate to keep mankind out of their grasp, an atomic fusion warhead was launched at the largest concentration of the Helgrammaw. The forces in power assumed the radiation would annihilate the invaders. They were right, to a point. They gained three years of frail peace at the cost of destroying a chunk of the world while radiation poisoned the areas within and beyond. When the Helgrammaw inevitably returned, they used more warheads. The result was the razing of their own civilization, but the creatures remained.

"Do you think it's safe, even with the radiation?" she asked

When curiosity was fresh, robots and cameras were sent first until it was realized that no amount of technology functioned in their presence. Then, military researchers, scientists, explorers, or anyone interested, attempted to explore the cordoned areas where the creatures lived. When none of them returned, the military were sent in to fight. When they lost and the area grew exponentially, the sitting president decided to release a nuclear warhead. The Helgrammaw adapted to that, too.

Madeline could not help but think of the baby, now a precocious young boy. Without Fiona's stubborn resolve, that child would have been left to suffer. Without Madeline's own resolve, that same child would have been left to wither. It was too easy to surrender to it all. She felt the fear as much as any other like a sudden flash of terror.

It was important to keep living, despite the insanity of the world. She smiled at the nickname bestowed on her.

If I'm "Mad" for fighting against insanity, who is sane?

Madeline picked up the telephone near her bed. Her finger hovered over the dial, then realized that she did not have contact information for her family beyond the letters they had sent. She hung up the receiver. Madeline got out of bed, went through the door, and down the hall.

"Hey," came a voice. It was one of the nurses.

Madeline kept walking even as the nurse caught up to her.

"Going somewhere?" he asked.

"My room."

"Ah," he said. "It seems you're going backwards." He pointed to her hospital room door with his thumb. "It's back that way."

"Nope," she said, continuing onward to the exit door.

"I don't think you'll have much success," he warned.

She came to the double doors and pushed but the doors stayed closed.

"You need to scan a pass," he said.

Madeline then noticed the black rectangular sensor with a red illuminated circle in the center on the wall adjacent to the door. She groaned.

"Okay. So, open this door," she demanded.

"No can-do," he said with an intonation that grated her nerves.

She turned around and glared at the nurse. He wore a uniform of similar colors as hers but wore an unfamiliar patch. Aside from his graying auburn hair there was nothing remarkable about him. His face, too, was one that she suspected was easily forgotten.

"Look, just open the door. I'll go to my room, come back, and it'll be fine," she said.

The nurse twisted his face into an expression that she could not define. She knew she had seen something like it before, but the memory and the classification of it was gone.

"If there's something you need, we can get it for you," he explained softly.

The thought of someone else touching her letters made her angry.

"No," she said with a raised voice. "I don't see why it's a problem for me to go to my room for a minute."

"It's not a problem for *you*; it's a problem for *me*," he said. "Gotta follow the regs."

"Not if they don't make any sense," she grumbled.

He laughed.

"You haven't been in the military for very long, have you?"

Madeline did not care for his condescension.

"I know more about it than you do," she said. "How many sixteen-year olds do you know that have done what I've done?"

They stood in the hallway staring at each other while Madeline waited for him to open the door.

"Forget it," she said and walked back down the hallway.

As soon as she returned to her hospital room, she laid down to sleep.

12

Madeline awoke to the glow of an afternoon sun. There was an ache in her arm that made it difficult to sit up. She reached over to massage the tightness in her muscles and was met with the empty space where her arm should be. Though her bladder was full, she tried to ignore it so she could remain in the bed for as long as possible. In the end, the pressure forced her to the bathroom. Once finished, she stood and looked around her room.

The room was adorned with medical equipment, a television that she thought would be pointless to try watching, and a desktop computer. With nothing else to do, she turned on the computer and sat in front of it. To her surprise, it worked, and was even connected to the internet. She sat there, staring at the screen, at the search bar that appeared on her browser. She had not considered before how the Mites emerged. At the time, it seemed useless to know. It had not mattered to her why or how they came to be, only that they existed and must be eradicated. That singular mindset was the fire that fueled her to survive the Ashfall, the refugee camp, military training, and all of the fighting. It was unfair that it should be extinguished so soon.

Before, there had been no time to think, to consider their creation. At the hospital, all she had was time. And there she sat for hours, reading, watching videos, researching what they were. So much and so little was known. The first instance of one of them appearing was seventy-five years before the Ashfall. It was a short video of one of the Mites on a beach. It was considered an oddity. A new deep-sea creature, perhaps. Then more emerged elsewhere. Then twenty years later was the first sighting of a Damocles Sphere. It was smaller than what existed now. Efforts were made to capture one, to dissect one. It had been impossible until, by luck or malevolent design, a dead one washed up on a shore.

Madeline had seen the dissection photos in her brief training. Knowing about their biology helped them understand how to fight them, but not how they thought. This was when they received their name: Helgrammaw. Madeline then learned that naming them "Helgrammaw" was poetic. With her human eyes, the creatures were black and terrifying, but when they touched her, when she was briefly in their minds as much as they were in hers, she saw their world from a new perspective. It was a primordial world free of human destruction and hope.

A disturbing thought spread from a dark place in the stem of her mind. Perhaps the Helgrammaw were beautiful, and her humanity prevented her from seeing it. Perhaps they deserved the Earth more than her brethren.

What have we done to deserve the Earth? She thought.
Maybe it's just luck.

She almost expected an alert from her phone to call her to another cache. Yet there was nothing except for the sounds of the cockroaches outside trilling their chirps into the sky. It was unnaturally quiet. She did not trust it.

Her eye opened to the white room around her. A memory returned. The piercing scream of the air breaking around her clattered around her ears. The suffocating stench of dust and heat stuck to her skin in a gritty sweat that she could never clean. And the slimy alien flesh crept up her arm. She remembered little else. Trying to recall the events that brought her here resulted in emptiness, as if parts of her brain had been lobotomized. That sound came to her again. With it, flashes in her vision. Even though she knew she could still fight, she wondered if the desire was truly there.

The door opened. In came a nurse with a slim digital tablet in one hand and pushed a metal cart with the other. On the cart was a spread of various medical supplies in front of him. The noise of the wheels grinding against the tile floor gave Madeline a sudden headache.

"Got a few things for you now that you're up," he said.

He picked up a stack of letters from the cart and gave them to her. At first elated, she took them at once. Then, upset at the breach of privacy, accused him, "You went through my things."

"Just the drawer."

"You broke in."

"Nah. I'm not that clever. I just called the building manager to open the door."

"Is that legal?"

"When you're on the government's dime, it is. Anyway, I thought it was the best way to get you what you wanted."

Madeline pressed her lips together and mumbled, "Thanks."

"There's something else," he said, tapping the cart.

On the same tray was an artificial arm. She half expected it to be a bulky plastic apparatus, but when she picked it up, she was surprised by the lightweight biomechanical artificial arm and the intricacies of the hand and fingers.

"Let me try it on," Madeline said.

She sat back down on the chair, only to be redirected to the bed. The nurse moved his finger around on the surface of the tablet and then set it down on the cart. He removed the bandages as gently as possible but the adhesive from the bandages pulled at her tender skin. The remains of her arm were patchworked. Some areas were thin and red while others had the pockmarked indentations of a skin graft. The end of the stump where they gathered the skin and sewed it together had healed. At the center were six round vein-blue electrical nodules.

The nurse fitted the limb on by attaching the base to the nodules in her arm. Madeline gasped. It was as if she had never lost a limb. The sensations when she rotated her hand were the same as if it were her own. She touched the artifice, smooth, and knocked against it with a closed fist. The trilling in her ears made her shake her head.

"Amazing, isn't it?" the nurse said.

Madeline stretched the arm outwards, opened and closed her fists, and wriggled her fingers. She smiled at the ingenuity.

"I guess you're not so bad," she said to the nurse.

He furrowed his brows. "Well, thank you."

The nurse tapped on the digital tablet and then took a pink rubber ball from his pocket and placed it on the bed.

"Try to pick this up,"

Madeline reached over and did so effortlessly. She squeezed it and tossed it against the adjacent wall so that it bounced back to her, and she caught it in both hands.

"Seems good to go," the nurse said

Through the door came a new doctor who held a small steel case in hand. As soon as he entered, the nurse handed the doctor the tablet and left. The doctor placed the case on the metal cart that the nurse had brought in.

"How is it?" he asked.

"Great," Madeline said.

The doctor checked the entirety of her arm then fiddled with the tablet.

"It looks like you're healing well. Keep it up and you'll be back home by next week."

"What? What do you mean 'back home'?" she asked.

"Medical discharge. Didn't they mention it?"

She tried to remember. Her troops and her supervising officers had come to see her. They gave her medals. There had been more.

Why can't I remember?

She stood up too quickly. Her head became dizzy for a moment, and she swayed but regained her posture.

"I'm healthy. I want to re-enlist," she said. "I don't even care if it's infantry."

"You're not listening. You're unauthorized."

She tightened her fists.

"I'm as capable as anyone."

"Are you?"

His questioning of her character made her meet his gaze with a determined stare.

"The standards now are that any who've made intimate contact with the Helgrammaw is automatically denied."

Intimate contact. She did not like the description.

"There's a reason for it.," he explained. "You're not the first I've seen." He lowered his voice. "You're hearing them, aren't you?"

"No--" she started, then stopped. If he knew, then there were more like her. "I mean . . . I don't know."

"It happens often enough. Sometimes people are fine, and others, not. The nurse said you looked at your scans."

"They looked fine to me."

He took a deep breath and exhaled.

"Your frontal lobe and amygdala have all the increased activity that signals interference from *them*. You go back into combat . . . It's too risky."

Madeline tried to process what he was saying.

"But," he said with a raised tone, "away from them, you'll re-integrate just fine. You're young. You have your whole life ahead of you."

Madeline huffed.

"Yeah, that's what my teachers used to tell me. It's not that helpful when you don't know what you want." Madeline rubbed her sore eye. "Since the Ashfall, I knew what I wanted to do. I knew that I had to get rid of them all. But now. . ." she trailed off and shrugged.

"It takes time," he said in a calm, parental tone.

"To do what?" she asked harshly.

"To grow into who you are."

She grimaced.

"I know who I am," she said proudly, though it was only a half-truth.

The doctor, unconvinced, narrowed his eyes then relaxed. He nodded once and put down the tablet.

"Then let's get that tracker out of you," he said.

"Wha--" Madeline started but stopped to process what he meant. She had forgotten about the device implanted under her skin. The doctor briefly pressed the pad of his thumb against the center of the case. There was a high-pitched tone and the case clicked. When he opened the case, the doctor removed a white oblong object with a short handle. On the handle was a digital display and two buttons below it, one blue and one red. The doctor then took out another object from the case contained inside medical packaging. He placed it next to her. The doctor instructed Madeline to lift her sleeve, which she did. He pushed the button and began hovering the object over her shoulder in slow circles. When it beeped, he pushed the red button, which left a similarly colored dot in its place.

Next, the doctor put on a pair of blue latex gloves. He picked up a small packet the size of a restaurant moist towelette, tore it open, and withdrew the square sponge inside.

"This will disinfect and numb the area," he said as he rubbed the marked area on her arm with the sponge. Madeline's skin pricked at the coldness.

With the doctor so close to her, Madeline tried to read his name tape, but she could only decipher the last few letters.

The doctor removed the gloves and replaced them with a fresh pair that he pulled from a dispenser on the cart. Next, he tore open the medical package that was inside the case and he took out the object.

"Looks like a stapler," Madeline said upon seeing it, which caused the doctor to chuckle.

The device looked like the one the recruiter had used to first insert the GPS tracker. It was a white plastic instrument with a thick top and a base in which the front half had a long needle attached to a handle. The doctor held it in his right hand. With his left hand he used his thumb and forefinger to stretch the skin.

"Ready?" he asked.

"Sure."

Madeline felt pressure as he inserted the needle. When he reached a certain point, he stopped, straightened the object, and squeezed the handle. He removed the instrument. At the insertion site there was blood. After setting the device on the cart, he took a cotton ball to absorb the blood and taped it in place with a single strip of brown adhesive. Madeline let her sleeve drop. She looked at the cart where she saw the bloody needle.

"Can I see it?" she asked.

"Absolutely," he said.

The doctor turned his back and when he faced her again, she saw that his name tape read "Miranda". In his gloved hand was a tiny white cylinder splotched with blood as small and thin as a paperclip. She held out her hand and he dropped it in her palm. It was nearly weightless. She rolled her fingers inward to feel it.

"I'll leave you to your letters," he said.

He left, taking the cart with him. Madeline looked at the stack of letters sitting on her bed and began re-reading them.

She wanted to see her family. Still, there was a cautious anxiety that made her want to avoid it. She had changed, and so had they. She knew her parents would ask her about the fighting, and she would not want to speak the answers. They would expect the same girl who left, not the young woman who returned. And before she saw them again, there was a journey still to be made.

13

adeline would go herself. She knew she might die but she would rather kill herself before becoming one of them. It was a risk. They could transform her while she walked in their midst. The sounds in her mind threatened to overtake her remaining logic. But she was increasingly determined to see the cordoned area, to destroy as many as she could. She had to go. Despite how people would convince her otherwise, there were others, more insidious, whispering to bolster her own determination.

No border marked the entry to the exclusion zone. There was no need for one. No sane person would seek out their territory. Without the special breathing equipment she had bought, no person would be able to withstand the environment for long. It was not just the oxygen levels, but there was also something else in the air that caused a change. It was the particles in the air she once mistook for snow. It was as if she were underwater with specks of plankton and debris floating in the air.

There was also the radiation. There was no way to know how much there was. All she knew for certain was that a warhead had detonated here to stop their growth. Perhaps the weapon had made them stronger, more resilient. She could not know, and it didn't matter to her. They were here now, and she wanted to see them.

A printed map of the area was her only way of navigation. The straightest path was by the county zoo. Going around would add hours. It was a risk. Everything she tended to do was a risk. But her legs were sore from walking, and she would rather take the most direct path than linger in the cordoned place. Only the darkened sky, the hazy sheen that covered the horizon, was a warning of their presence. It was an eerie silence that signaled she had arrived. Her expectation that there would be guards to stop anyone from entering was false. There was not even a warning sign, except for the absence of human noise. There was no need for any of these; the nearest human settlement was thousands of miles away and there were too few of them to waste on standing guard duty. The small number who joined the fight were used to push back the offense.

The humid air made it feel as if she were walking through oil. The sky was saturated and murky. The low buzzing in her ear elevated. In time, she would have to become accustomed to it so she could ignore the interception. It became like any other natural sound, no different from the chirping cockroaches.

She had been wearing a mask, but unease made her check that it was secure. The eeriness of the exclusion zone was in its uncanny normalcy in certain areas and razed buildings in others. On the edge were pristine homes with overgrown lawns, trash cans still on the edge of the driveway waiting to be received, weathered flags on poles, abandoned vehicles. Interspersed were bulbous, smooth urchins, ranging from small to enormous sizes, their surface as a glass reflection. A fine breeze caused the urchins to quiver and their skin to harden into an opaline sheen as the breeze passed over.

Madeline stepped close to one basking in the lush grass, so close that she could see the internal veins through the translucent flesh. It looked familiar somehow. She reached out a finger to touch it curiously but stopped at the bombardment of a memory. Madeline had touched one of these before. She knew at once that it was a Mite.

It can't be, she thought. And yet, scrutinizing it presented the truth.

What she had witnessed on the battlefield had been limited to her human perception. Everything that was once recognizable was changed, some in the subtlest of ways. There was grass but it was softer, and wet, as if drenched from a monsoon and never dried. The ruins of neighborhoods were there and yet different. They had been overtaken by puffy algae and colorful barnacles. It all seemed to have softness to it. She resisted the curious instinct to touch it with her naked fingers.

She followed the trail as she passed the remnants overtaken by the Helgrammaw. The broken homes and dilapidated neighborhoods were the shells of comfort destroyed by friendly bombs in attempts to eliminate the creatures who nevertheless survive.

There are too many places like this, she lamented.

Yet she had never seen an area so lush with life. It was a breathing sea forest that survived on land. Bizarre shapes that were innocuous underwater transform the surface into an alien world. It was hardly a recognizable earth. Had she not walked into the boundary from her place amongst civilization, there would be no way to judge its origin.

Opaque mucus covered the ground. From it emerged rock sponges. Rusted street signs were covered with fluorescent lichen while others bent from the weight of the alien vegetation. Tall mushroom-like beings reached higher than the ruined business towers. Tiny sea pods and urchins crept along unperturbed. There were Mites, too, hundreds of them, though they did not show aggression as they might have in past encounters. In fact, nothing had.

Movement made her flinch. There was a lumbering jelly-like creature a dozen meters or so in front of her. It wandered along, unaware of or unconcerned with her presence. Another being passed in front of Madeline. This one was lithe, tall, and walked as if its feet slid across the ground. It reminded her of a dancer. It kept to one side of the street on what Madeline assumed was an old sidewalk, though it was similarly covered in the vibrant green vegetation. The creature walked and then stopped.

If it has eyes, it's looking at me, she thought.

She could fight it, but then what? A threat to one would alert them all. And, thus far, none of the Helgrammaw had been aggressive to her presence. Her heart beat and she clenched her fists. The dancer made an odd movement of the arms, as if to raise them, and then abruptly ceased. It then turned to a particular house on the street that was a mass of lichen with hundreds of mushrooms growing on the roof and pink eel-like animals poking out of the vinyl siding.

Madeline could stare at the house for hours.

Remember why you're here, she thought.

She looked around for a sign for the zoo and found it obscured by lichen. She walked past it. In the empty space were vibrant green mounds. One after another, the mounds lined the sidewalks. She went towards one of them and pulled the plant matter away. It was moist and left a residue on the material underneath. It was a car. All the mounds were cars. Families that had wanted to have a day of fun had disappeared. All those people would have become Helgrammaw.

Maybe the dancer was one of them.

The main entrance was unlocked. The door was heavy with the overgrowth, and it took two hands to pull it open. Some of the vegetation had crept under the door, but for the most part it was clear. Still, she would not remove her protection. There was risk and there was stupidity. Seeing the gift shop, the main ticket counter, and children's school backpacks made her pause. She had actively avoided thinking about the day the Ash fell. She and her family survived, remained human, but there were thousands, perhaps millions who had not, and she had not considered that a majority of them would have been children. Her stomach lurched and she forced down the sickness that bubbled up her throat.

She would not go in.

Despite her discomfort, Madeline turned and walked the walls around the zoo. There were noises that sounded from within; Trills and undulations that mimicked the tempo of birds and wild animals. She stopped periodically to rest. She rubbed the soreness around the amputation. The artificial arm assisted in her recovery, but the difference in weight distribution still took some time to adjust. After some time, she stood up and continued walking.

There were dim spheres along the path. When she touched one, her fingers slipped over the slick moisture covering the surface. She prodded and found it viscous. Shadows behind a window drew her attention. When she pushed her fingers against it, the surface bent inwards under the pressure until she could pass through. The substance left a sheen that covered her body. When she looked behind her, the wall moved like ripples across the surface of a tide pool. The entire interior seemed to breathe. The origin came from clusters of Helgrammaw settled within what appeared to be masses of seabed coral covered by brightly colored plant life that she recognized as endemic to an ocean reef. Pearlized vegetation grew in the darker corners beneath hues of brackish teal. The Mites sprouted from translucent stems swaying in an unseen wave. Glowing blue mushrooms emitted ultraviolet light from the ribs and underside cap. She half expected to see fish swim through the bits of plant grass.

Madeline felt water in her ears. Her hair prickled. She was reminded of swimming underwater in a crowded pool where limbs and legs paddled, causing residual waves to push her outward.

There must be a central mind here.

The Helgrammaw floated as if they were as natural as clouds. The soundless creatures drifted with their pulsating long tendrils that she could reach up and touch. She expected them to attack her. With each step she became more paranoid. Her experience with them was rooted in violence. Her memories of them were colors of aggression. They were a continual procession of enemies in the way of humanity. It was strange to see them in a state of peaceful silence.

One began to change color from a pale pastel to a golden orange with violet circles. Large fractal eyes covered by a thin mucous film stared at Madeline. The creature had a gelatinous membrane that seemed to move of its own accord. Its head was enlarged with ears and tentacles growing where a nose and mouth should have been. When it spoke, it was not with a mouth, but with the skin. Colors, ripples, patterns moved in ways that she could barely begin to understand. This was a language that could not be communicated through tongue. What reconciliation could there be between species that were incapable of basic communication? It was as if trying to explain morality to a squid.

The nonsensical trilling that had been noise to Madeline before began to take a calmer tone. She listened. There was a logic to it that presented in the form of colors and immediate understanding. Her own human forms of communication seemed crude in comparison. Complex emotions, thoughts, ideals, were all determined by how well a person could use their tongue and throat to manipulate sound. With the Helgrammaw, these things were understood immediately through hues, waves, colors, and vibrations to form a perfect expression.

They sang to her as if in a lullaby. Words were unnecessary to fully comprehend when the melody was so clear. Blues and pinks warbled amongst other colors that had no description on her visual spectrum. She imagined them as synapses; biological streams which she could follow and comprehend their universal meaning.

Why couldn't I see it before?

She could not distinguish whether or not the creature she stared at had been male or female.

What are you called? she wondered.

The answer came as soon as she conceived the question.

We.

The labels she gave them: Helgrammaw, Damocles Spear, Mites, eggs, creatures. Such monikers were unnecessary to them. It was a sentient, conscious mind that was paramount. They did not change those who did not wish it. She thought of the old woman, Dubrovin, on her first day afield, or her friend Juniper, who she assumed became one of them by force. An intrusive memory appeared for her to focus upon. It was her own on the day she feared her humanity was changing. How she fought against it, even as she saw the heavenly world ascending. And when she fought, they relented. They wouldn't change anyone who didn't want it.

Madeline's stomach lurched.

It was all pointless, she thought. *All the fighting, the death. It meant nothing.*

The buzzing grew stronger. She shook her head as if to get water out of her ears. Why had she been fighting? It seemed she had been so sure before. Now, that steadfastness dissipated. The sounds that had been so penetrable, so at odds with her mind, spilled out. She had thought of them as voices, but that was not what they were. They were thoughts. She could not feel her body, her face, or her legs. Everything dematerialized until all she had was her mind.

Shining lights of reds and whites emerged on the horizon. A great spire stood in the center with a shining red light on top. In her upper peripherals, she noticed the clouds form into a dull green like the sky before a tornado. Particles fell but she was not afraid. They drifted as gently as autumn flurries.

Madeline heard them before she saw them. She knew what they were and looked at them with new understanding. The Mites were in states of transformation. Some were more human than others until the particles touched their skin. There, Madeline witnessed a metamorphosis. Bulky forms became slender. Their new bodies were beautiful and angelic like the opalescent dancer.

A loud whistle cracked against Madeline's eardrums, and she suddenly felt as if she had been doused with a bucket of icy water. She fell into a descent from an adrenaline high into a dreamless sleep with only the blackness around her and the sense that she was not asleep at all but merely between worlds. There was comfort in the silence, as if she felt immediately taken with it.

If only to sleep, if only to sleep.

The voices became sensations. Their silent melodies were reverberations felt upon the skin. There was peace here. She felt a quiet evolution. It was as if she had submerged into a still hot spring pool. At first there was tension as the skin retracted from the initial heat. Then she slowly relaxed to accept the immense comfort of the new water. In the depths were thoughts. A thousand, a hundred thousand, she could not know for certain. All of them existed in a harmonious symbiosis within the new world.

Madeline could stay. She could remove her mask, her suit, breathe in the Ash, and relinquish humanly troubles. The business of living was hard. It was a constant fight, and she was tired. The creatures tempted her to peace. There was no pain in their bodies, no sorrow, no struggle. When her mind touched theirs, there was only an immense, inexplicable joy, free from her mortal skin.

Is this what heaven feels like? she wondered.

Madeline could stay forever in that consciousness, floating unhindered in a tranquil ocean. There would be no more struggle.

What's the point of it?

She knew there was a reason, lost somewhere in her disappearing mind. She searched for it, stubbornly, against the desire for peace. She had been sure before. There was an enemy, a clear enemy, that she had seen eviscerate her human brethren. Again, she thought of the old woman whose body was mauled and maimed beyond recognition, and of Rostein, Goodway, and herself, and the countless others before her who all carried the enemy's mark. What the Helgrammaw did to them was the temptation to relinquish humanity. She wanted to let go, to welcome the ethereal songs that coaxed her onward. Yet, a miniscule part of herself would not submit. It nagged at her from a primordial center in her brain.

It was not an image, nor a memory, but a feeling. The warmth of familial comfort. The smell of a mother's skin. A father's tempered breathing. A baby's coo. A sister's joy.

It pulled her from tranquility.

It was as if she woke from a feverish sleep. The malaise passed and birthed a new clarity. Madeline turned and walked away. She slipped past the creatures, careful not to touch them. They turned their heads to the sky, waiting for the ash to touch their twisted skin, and when it did, their flesh dissipated, replaced by a phosphorescent glow. A stillness emerged when metamorphosing from their grotesque amalgamation to that of the ethereal.

She walked, all the time feeling the pull, knowing that they were there, waiting for her, in the distance, and in the confines of her mind. But her humanity was worth more. Humanity that she wanted to keep. No matter how hopeful, no matter how grim, it was worth fighting for. It was sacred.

14

Outside beyond the smudged car window panes was an endless grassy plain uprooted by mountains and spotted with trees. She rolled down her windows to breathe in the sylvanian air; bushy evergreens whose wild fragrance wafted in the breeze, or a waterfall whose fresh mountain stream trickled down a rock face. Madeline and her sister took turns behind the wheel of a well-used Jeep. When baby Eli began to cry, they would stop to pull into a rest area.

Madeline took the chance to smoke a cigarette. In the open space, she reflexively put a hand on the knife attached to her belt and watched as Fiona tended to Eli. When Madeline came closer, Fiona scolded her to wash her hands and change her shirt before touching Eli, saying that the smoke was not good for him. Madeline complied. Less than halfway through the trip and she was nearly through all her clean shirts.

While they drove, Fiona did most of the talking. Through it, Madeline was pleased to learn how her money had helped secure their lodgings. A two-bedroom apartment that was small but enough for them. Her parents had found service work, and Fiona was studying to complete her General Education Diploma. Being displaced from public education, it was her only option in lieu of finishing High School.

"We'll have to make space for you now," Fiona said. "We'll share a room, like we did before."

"We always ended up fighting," Madeline answered.

"Ah, we were kids," she dismissed. "Things are different now. I've got Eli. I don't have time for stupid little fights."

Madeline warmed at the idea. It would be nice to live amongst her family again.

At an indiscriminate point, marked only by a small wooden sign painted with a red arrow, they turned into a bumpy dirt road where there was a camp of log cabins and a large stable. Fiona parked off the side of the road and into the grass. With their bags in tow, Fiona carried Eli in one arm, and she headed towards a log cabin with a weathered bench on the short porch. Fiona knocked on the door and it soon opened. On the other side were her mother and father.

Madeline found herself unable to move. From a distance, they seemed like strangers welcoming her sister and child with hugs and kisses. Fiona turned and waved at Madeline. Somehow, Madeline could not seem to move her feet. She started in disbelief at who they had become, looking altogether changed from when she had last seen them. Both parents rushed towards her. Her mother's long hair whipped in the air and around her shoulders. Her father opened his arms wide. Both parents grabbed her in an unrelenting hug. Her mother pressed her cheek so closely that Madeline felt her cheekbones and smelled her clean hair that had soaked in a warm sun and pine tree pollen. Madeline found that her own arms were wrapped tightly around her mother, refusing to let go.

Her mother wiped tears from her eyes, pulled away, and looked at her daughter. Her mother's hand went to the chain around Madeline's neck and pulled it out gently to reveal the pendant.

"Mom," Madeline said gently, wanting to say more and not knowing what.

As if in silent answer, her mother shook her head. She smiled and her eyes were as crescent moons.

"Oh," she said, sniffling, "Oh, I missed you."

Madeline felt a crack inside her. Her lips quivered. She did not stifle her tears. Her mother stroked her hair, and whispered, "It's okay." There they stayed until she purged the tears from her eyes. When she finally pulled away, her eyesight was red and blurry.

"When did you get this?" her mother asked, looking down at Madeline's artificial arm.

Madeline's answer was interrupted by her father's embrace. He gripped her tightly, and she remained caught between the two of them, unable to move. Madeline began to feel the uncomfortable pressure of their weight. She wriggled. At the notice of her discomfort, her father backed away. When he did, she noticed the tears rolling down his cheeks that he wiped away with the back of his hand. Madeline looked away.

Memories tumbled into the forefront of her mind. The crying baby without a parent, the disaster relief vans, visiting military recruiters, and then her parents begging her to stay with them.

I shouldn't have gone, she thought. *Maybe it was all a mistake.*

"I'm sorry," she said.

"For what?"

"I--You were right. I should have been with you instead of joining."

"No," her mother said immediately. "*We* were wrong. You did what you thought was the right thing to do. Without you, where would we be?"

Madeline's gaze shifted from her mother's eyes, to her father, to her sister walking next to Eli and catching him when he stumbled. This was where she had chosen to be.

Still, she heard the distant buzz and a hiss behind her ears.

15

adeline tossed in her sleep. The quilts wound around her body, and she was trapped by them. She breathed quickly, even whispered as she dreamed. Behind her eyelid, she saw a flash of fire before her and the expulsion of dirt into the air. Carousing in her ears was the sound of flesh tearing, bones breaking, and Mites buzzing. She could not stop the visions despite her efforts.

Once her eye snapped open, Madeline sat up. Her head was dizzy. The room spun around her, and she could not hold on to where she was. Taking a deep breath, she sat up and rubbed her eye with her hand. It did nothing to relieve the soreness that emerged. She got up to retrieve her eye drops and squeezed a drop in her eye. Relieved, Madeline walked out into the sitting room. She left her prosthetic on the bedside table where she had removed it before falling asleep.

Madeline passed Fiona's room, which had its door half-open. Quiet breathing came from within. One she recognized as her sister's and the other was Eli's. She peeked in and smiled when she saw her sister sleeping on her back, an arm over her eyes, and baby Eli cuddled next to her. Her parent's room door was closed, but she could hear her father snoring.

Madeline stood by a window where the soft glow of dawn filled the room. A twittering birdsong made her pause. She recognized it as a robin's call and waited for the bird to make an appearance. Fiona walked drowsily over to her, wordlessly, and hugged her.

"I forgot what they looked like," Madeline said. "I haven't seen a bird in..." she paused, trying to think. "I don't remember."

When the bird appeared, Madeline took a sharp inhale in awe at the robin flicking its tail feathers. Fiona glanced out the window, then to Madeline, and inevitably, to the missing limb.

"I missed you," her sister said.

Madeline had never been told that by her sister. When things had been normal, they were never away from each other long enough to be missed. An emotional swell threatened tears. These past years, she had no time for crying. Madeline tried to blink the tears away from her eye. Crying happened during calm. Despite her efforts, the overwhelming cascade forced her to submit. Tears sprouted from her eye, rolling down the sides of her nose and over her upper lip.

Fiona joined her in quiet whimpers, streaming tears, and the occasional sniffling.

Madeline wiped her face. She rummaged through her bags and then found what she was looking for. She returned to her sister and presented the black cases. Fiona opened them.

"Keep them," Madeline said.

Fiona looked at the medals, then back at Madeline. "No," she said, "they're yours; you earned them."

Madeline scrunched her face in repugnance. "I don't want them."

"What are you saying? When have you ever gotten anything like this? *You* keep them."

Madeline grimaced. "No. It's not worth it. I don't need a shiny medal to tell me I did my job." Madeline then thought of the reason she went to war in the first place. Seeing the baby asleep in the other room, she said. "What about Eli?"

At the mention of him, Fiona looked at the sleeping child, then to her sister, and nodded in concession. Fiona took the medals.

"He would've died if you hadn't--" her voice wavered and she exhaled to steady it, "--I should've done it."

Madeline laughed.

"You were stronger than I was. I couldn't stay there taking care of everyone. I was never any good at that kind of stuff." Madeline looked up to the ceiling, as if searching for stars. "Maybe I can do that now."

Her sister nodded slightly. She was about to say something when the sounds of Eli stirring drew her attention away.

Darkness in a Sky of Embers

Early morning brought the unmistakable lumbering of a bear outside of the cabin, just far enough to keep her from fear but close enough so that she dared not make a sound. She watched as it turned its paws outward to walk around the area, holding its head up to smell the air. It appeared harmless. The great bear swayed through their small plot of civilization, passing by those who slept soundly without so much as a grunt. It made Madeline aware that she was in the wild. It was a place that was never far from the face of a buffalo or the call of a wolf. One step too close to a buck and her life would be at the mercy of the animal's reach. There was an awesome sight to be had when surrounded by such wilderness, but it was not a sight to ignore for a moment. She looked to the morning sky where she could still see some stars. There was a constellation before her that she recognized but could not name. They were so close that she could almost reach out and pluck them.

The untouched wilderness was as beautiful as it was unforgiving. Instinct drove her to walk amongst it. She put on her adaptive arm and dressed warmly. Yet, when she reached the door of her bedroom, she stopped, removed the arm, and placed it gently on the bed. Upon opening the front door, Madeline took a deep breath to let the unspoiled air permeate her lungs.

There were birds warbling in the trees and rustling in the leaves. Unable to resist her curiosity, Madeline reached out to touch her palm to the coagulated trunk of the tree. She was surprised by the roughness of its surface that she imagined was the consistency of a horned lizard's skin. She stroked the bark with her thumb, sure that if she applied enough pressure it would cut into her flesh. She took her hand away from the sparkling substance that oozed its way from within the trunk.

Madeline touched a finger to it and felt the sticky afterbirth of its sap. She raised the strange ooze to her nose and smelled it. It was like no other scent that she had been exposed to for years, the very essence of it, the blood of the pine, the smell of it she could remember from a broken memory. When she tried to rub it off, it left a filmy residue that refused to disappear. The sap remained stuck to her finger until it was covered with a film of grime and became smooth. The wind blew in against her face. A great joy overwhelmed her at the sound of the rushing air funneling through her ears and the *swish* of her feet against the grass as she walked.

Madeline stopped at the sight of the crystalline lake in the distance. It rippled in the early morning. A splash of water from an unseen animal beneath the surface appeared near the far edge of the lake. There was life here that she only vaguely remembered. Each colorful animal stole away within the stilted woods and tall grasses as she approached the lake shore.

At the edge of the water, Madeline squatted to put her hand in, surprised at the frigid temperature, and the crispness of it on her skin. Her deep exhaustion: every stress in her life weighed heavy on her. A cool breeze carried with it the scent of a millennia of wilderness. She stood at the edge of the lake in the soft grass of the meadow and peered into its abyss. In the shallow pools surrounding the crevices there were tiny Cutthroat Trout darting about in the placid pools. Madeline hunched over to see her wavy reflection mirrored in the water. A rush of mucous-like liquid pooled inside her eardrums.

Without a thought, she plunged her head into the chill water. The fish scattered. She shuddered in response to the glacial water as her clothes flowed with the soft current. She opened her eye in the murky water where ancient pebbles resided in the catchment. Once her breath ran out, she pulled her face away and inhaled deeply, taking the icy air into her lungs until her entire body shook from the cold.

She felt awakened, as if every pore in her body suddenly breathed in life for the first time. She plunged her face into the water once more. She held it there until it became numb to the cold. All she could hear was the muffled sound of swirling water around her. The trills and the thoughts that should be voices would never leave her. In a single action, she opened her mouth to let the shrill water dance around her tongue. In an act of mindlessness, she breathed in. Her body refused it immediately, convulsing and vomiting to keep her from drowning. Madeline pushed herself up and gasped. She sucked in the dry air around her.

A white doe appeared from down the hill and came ever closer. A fawn followed her until they stood only a few feet away from Madeline. The doe paused in her steps to assess her. After a moment, the animals continued forward until they came to the edge of the lake adjacent to Madeline. The doe dropped her head down and drank. Her fawn followed. It spread its legs awkwardly wide to dip its head down into the lake. The doe's ears twitched back and forth, listening for any sign of danger. She lapped up the water quietly. At times, an insect would land on the doe's back, but she did not move save for a twitch of her skin. When she lifted her head, Madeline could almost make out her reflection in the doe's eyes. The doe blinked once and turned away from the lake to show her remarkable profile. With graceful strides she walked silently onwards with her fawn in tow.

Madeline stood before the softened face of the valley and gazed at its beauty. In that moment where time seemed to leave her untouched, she felt benediction. Nothing was expected of her except to live and breathe. From the distance she heard a soothing melody emerge from the silence around her. It was the song of a thousand transient voices: the olden songs of nature descending upon her ears. There was a small freedom in the confines of those few minutes before the last of the starry night bled into the morning. The sun rose as a blazing light burning through the darkness in a sky of embers.

--End--

9 781951 768454